The **Suicide** Girls

KATIE KERCHNER

Trafford rev. 01/24/2014

 www.trafford.com

North America & international
toll-free: 1 888 232 4444 (USA & Canada)
fax: 812 355 4082

This book is dedicated to:

My parents and my sister who I took for granted all these years. I never really knew how lucky I had it until I saw how others lived. I am grateful to them for everything they have done for me and for always being there when I really needed them.

And to my fiancée who pushed and pushed for me to get this book published and out there for others to read.

A Special Thanks to:

Toni Koller, the best damn English teacher I could have wished for and who not only helped me to edit this book, but who also helped me become a better writer.

April 29th

Today is day one. Not the official day it was supposed to be, but the damn girl jumped the gun. She couldn't wait any longer, couldn't take the pressure. She ruined everything for me; it was all planned and she messed it up. I had to start this damn thing two days early. Calm down. Calm down. From now on it will be as planned.

May 1st

It's not right that today is so beautiful. The weather is just too perfect for this to be happening. The sky is so clear I can see for miles all around, not a cloud in sight. The late spring sun beats down on us, but an occasional breeze gave us respite from its heat. Usually when I picture a funeral I imagine a cold, damp rainy day, not some picture perfect day in May. Then again, I guess we can't choose our times, our places, or our lives. Well, most of us can't.

Sitting a few rows in front of me are her usually cold parents. I've never seen them smile or laugh. Her mother's stone cold face never moves, not even a glimmer of emotion. Her father is always rigid posture always makes him look invincible, like no one or nothing could bring him to tear down his guards. I almost thought I saw a tear in the corner of her mother's eye. But maybe the breeze just made them water. For the first time since I can remember, they didn't look so cold. Her father, a hard as nails cop, had a look of self-pity. HA! He blamed himself, well he should. They should all blame themselves. Her mother, a plastic surgery addict slash ex model, still had her solid face of dreamland on, but I could see in her eyes that she was crying inside too.

The rest of the crowd kind of just stood there in their own little worlds. Most of them were probably wondering why they were there, normal teenagers don't just kill themselves. Well for the select few of us who actually knew her, we knew it was coming.

Earlier today the school counselors had told our class that she probably did it because graduation was coming up and the thought of college and the "great unknown" was overwhelming. Well for your information, that's a bunch of crap. She wasn't afraid of college, she was just fed up with life, but aren't we all? To be honest though, only a few of us really know exactly why she did it. Yes, I'm one of those people. No, I'm not telling. You'll just have to figure it out yourself, or pay attention.

Anyway, back to a neutral subject, the weather. The sun is out, there's a warm breeze, and flowers are blooming. Like I said before, today is too perfect a day for a funeral. Though I guess it does match who she used to be. She used to be just as perfect as this weather, that was a few years ago, but that's not a neutral subject either, so I won't discuss it with you.

Looking at the girls faces to my left and right, I could tell that their minds wandered occasionally too. But just like me, none of them showed any emotions. Good girls, I'm proud of you.

As the funeral ended, everyone slowly began to get into their cars and head over to the diner.

Alicia questioned if we should go along with the crowd. I know we were all thinking the same thing. We'd have to sit there and listen to them complain and moan about how great she used to be and how badly she turned out. Not really my idea of fun. Then Isabella pointed out that there would be free food.

And that decided it for us. We were off to the diner for free food and talk of old times that should just be left alone. It's never a good thing when someone brings up god memories because with the good comes the bad and we wouldn't want to spoil their memories of a picture perfect girl.

As we walked into the doors of the diner we could immediately smell the wonderful greasy food of the restaurant. I could hear everyone talking about everything but our dead Ashlyn. People are so hesitant, so afraid to say dead. But face it, you will die and you can't stop that, so suck it up and just say it, she's dead.

The girls and I sat down at the far end of the table away from the parents and closer to the family outcasts and those random people who no one knows who probably only showed up for the free food (like us).

Once everyone finally got seated, the priest/preacher man (I never could tell the difference) stood up. "I would like to have a moment of silence for Ashlyn." Everyone got quiet and no one moved. After a few short seconds he began to speak again, first they all prayed; I don't pray; then he said, "Her parents have asked that we take a few minutes to talk about who she was and different things she might have done. Just some good memories."

Several people got up and pretty much said the same things. She was great, she was perfect, she was so beautiful; she was what everyone wanted her to be. Everyone talked about before; no one mentioned the last couple years.

Her grandmother stood up and as she spoke she looked at us. Everyone knew when we became friends that we had changed her in a way they didn't like and had ruined their life plan for her. "I was so proud of her in middle school, she was planning to be head cheerleader by the time she graduated high school, and I knew she really wanted to be a doctor of some sorts. Even though she took the wrong path in high school, I always have, and always will love her."

Okay whatever; keep staring at me you bitch. I'll admit that we did change her a bit, but it was for the best. She became what she never would or could have without me. If anyone in the family ever paid any attention to her, they would know that she used to be so miserable pretending to be happy and trying to become what her parents would want for her.

So, the girls and I sat there for a while, listening to everyone talk, but mostly complain about pointless things such as the horrible food, the government, and what each of them had been doing since they last got together.

"I am so bored," was all Stacey kept moaning.

"Alright, well then we will leave," I told them. And we did.

We went outside and sat on the hoods of our cars. Seven girls, four cars; some of the girls didn't have their licenses and some didn't want to get them. Or in the case of one who kept coming up with these bullshit excuses not to get it. This meant that the four of us who drove, had to drive far out of our way just to pick them up and haul their asses around.

What a party we were having. Oh yes, another thing for me to admit, I don't usually talk a lot (out loud), mostly I talk to you in this journal, to myself, and to my semi-best friend, Emily. She's not quite the best at listening, but she is one of the best at talking, so usually when I can't or won't talk, she fills in the silence. Even though there are eight, I mean, were eight of us, now seven, she and I were occasionally closer to each other than with the rest of them. I guess it's only right, since we did start this group and, as far as we know, we will end the group too.

So we kind of all just sat on our cars for a few minutes, staring off into space, then slowly the other girls left. We all had a few things to do before the night, so it only made sense to do them now instead of sitting there staring at each other.

I waited until Em and I were the last ones there and she moved over and stood by my car. No one but me sits on my car. I looked at her and said, "Do you think they will still do it? I mean after today, I wonder about some of them."

She looked at me and thought about the question. "I think that they will because they go before us, so really it's you and me I'm worried about."

To me, this made a lot of sense, but at the same time, it made no sense at all. I mean, if we are the ones who planned all this out, then why wouldn't we go through with it? Does that make any sense to you?

"Well my dear Em, if you do it, then I will too."

She just nodded her head at me. End of conversation, we both got into my car, and I drove 20 minutes out of my way to drop her off at home. Aren't I such a good person *gags*.

And so I ended up here, locked in my bedroom, writing this stuff down for you. My hopes in doing this are so that I may enlighten you, which I believe you really do need. Think of your own children, siblings, friends or even yourself. Everyone pushing you in the "right" direction: college, work, whatever the case may be. How do they know what the "right" direction is? How do they know how you really feel?

I can hear my mom downstairs cleaning the house, again. It's not like we don't have a cleaning lady to do the cleaning for us. She comes three times a week and does the same job every one of those days.

My mom's a neat freak and my dad's a surgeon. He's never home so she needs something to do, other than bother me of course. I do have a younger sister; younger by only three years, so I can't exactly call her my little sister since she's in high school too. We aren't very close. I'm not really sure why. We have some things in common such as . . . well I don't really know. I guess I really don't know much about her. Some days I wish that we were closer, best friends, and other days I don't because then we would fight like typical sisters, so I guess it's just better this way. I'm willing to bet that Amanda and I will never be closer than just saying hi as we pass in our kitchen. I guess I can't be too sad about that, can't be sad about losing something if you never had it, right?

Back to my original point, since I'm never home, and as far as I know, Amanda isn't either, and I know Dad is barely ever here, Mom needs to keep herself occupied, needs to forget her pathetic self-pity and needs to stop living in the past. Like Ashlyn's mother, my mother was a model too, but you can't stay young forever. Hence the reason she cleans and cleans and cleans some more; it gives her something to do, keeps her distracted. One good thing though, is that she never comes in my room; that is my personal space and she knows this, and I guess it's a very good thing she doesn't come in here.

We used to live about five houses down, but the house wasn't big enough for my dearest mother. Our house used to be able to have about seven people living comfortably there; this new one could hold about ten. The move was a surprise for both my father and me, we both came home really late one day to a completely empty house. Mom and Amanda were sitting inside on the stairs and explained to us that she had bought the house down the street, had bought some new furniture, packed all of our things and moved them into the new house. At the time I had nothing to hide from her, so I wasn't bothered by the fact that she packed and unpacked everything I owned, but now . . . if she was capable of feeling any emotions, she'd be furious if she knew anything true about me.

First off, the light pink room, which my mom had personally decorated for me, was now black, black walls and carpet, black everything. What? It's my favorite color! Saws, bolt cutters, chains and other various tools used to create chaos in our town were laying in plain view, and evidence of my alcoholic and smoking habits were apparent too. From where I sit now I can count at least two cases worth of empty beer bottles and four empty packs of cigarettes. All of which have accumulated in just the past week. The other thing is the tattoos and piercings, if my mom had actually taken a good look at me when I walked into the house, she would hardly even recognize me, but as usual, she doesn't even notice.

All the girls I hang out with have some form(s) of body art. Ashlyn's younger sister told me that when their parents found

Ashlyn's dead body; they were convinced that it wasn't their daughter. I admired that girl, she had more tattoos than I could count, well actually she only had 18 (one for every year she was alive), but that's still a lot. AND she had some piercings where I would never dare to put them. If her parents, or my parents, or any of our parents would pay attention to us, then we might not be where we are today. Ashlyn would still be alive and no one else would have to die.

Anyway, on another topic. So tonight the rest of us girls are going over to the school to do a little decorating. I call it art, others might call it graffiti. Whatever it is, graduation is coming up in a month and no one goes into the auditorium until the day before, which won't be enough time to find and then clean everything up. Our graduation should turn out to be one heck of an interesting night.

Well, in this little journal of mine, I will be talking a lot about my friends. So I guess it might be best to introduce them now, so there's no confusion later. There were eight of us. We were perfect, well we still are, but now we are one less. Let me name them: Alicia, Ashlyn, Brooke, Madison, Isabella, Stacey, Emily, and me. I guess we were all just meant to be together. Ashlyn and Alicia were very close, same with Brooke and Madison, Isabella and Stacey, and me and Em. Yeah, it's just meant to be.

Here's a little piece of information you might find interesting . . . when we became friends I made each of the girls tell me and only me; one deep, dark secret, which is very good for leverage and possible blackmail. I like to cover my ass. Which means that I have a piece of each and every one of them that puts them a little closer to me than to each other.

So, first we had Ashlyn, blonde hair, blue eyes, average height and weight, tattoos and piercings. Five foot seven inches, roughly 120 pounds, you average American teenager. She had piercings covering every inch of her ears, one in her lip and one in her eyebrow. A swastika tattoo on the back of her neck could only be seen when she wore her hair up in a bun and a scantily clad pin up girl took up the majority of her right forearm. A .45 caliber hand gun was held by a sinister looking man on her hip and the phrase 'Make War, Not Love' was written in calligraphy down her left calf. She was the quietest person of the group, now she's dead. Let's see; her parents (well all of our parents) never paid attention to her. It was Ash's theory that our parents probably assumed that once we hit high school, it wasn't necessary for them to help out with our lives anymore, or something like that. I actually never paid attention to her much, I mean she was beautiful and did everything we did or told her to do, but on the few occasions that she did talk, she was totally stupid, nothing that came out of her mouth was ever useful, so I tended to ignore her. I'm almost glad she's gone, though if she hadn't killed herself, I would have been the first in line to help her out. I'm pretty good at helping make deaths look like suicide; don't ask because I won't tell.

Second, we have Alicia, she was Ash's counterpart, and the two of them were usually found attached at the hip hiding behind a fashion magazine. Where Ash was quiet, Alicia is very talkative. It's hard to get any words in while she's talking, so I also wasn't as close to her either. Alicia is almost an exact replica of Ash; it's actually kind of weird. One difference between them was that Alicia has quite a few less tattoos and they are religious. A cross covered her entire back and the Lord's Prayer was written down her arm. Right now, Alicia is more into facial piercings than anything else. I guess if she fucks up her face now, she won't have long to worry about it because she's next to go. In junior high Alicia and Ashlyn were both planning on going to the same med school together and becoming doctors or nurses together. There is one major difference between the two of them which is that Ashlyn was an indoor type of person and the only outdoor activity she liked was swimming in her big ass pool, whereas Alicia is a farm girl. She has several horses and would probably spend hours riding them if she weren't busy with us.

Next we have Brooke and Madison, both a little bit closer to me, but still not as close as Emily. Let's start with Brooke. She is extremely skinny and a dancer or she used to be.

You will notice me say, "Used to" a lot, because sometimes it's hard to believe that times have changed and that things are so much better now. I probably have the worst attention span of anyone you will ever meet.

Back to Brooke, seeing as that she was such a good dancer she tended to favor exotic tattoos that showed off as she moved around. The flower tattoos on her shoulders waved and flowed as though a phantom breeze was causing them to blow back and forth. The dragon on her lower back was intimidating. When she twisted to the left or right I swear real flames were going to shoot out of its mouth. Madison on the other hand, was the one who followed Brooke around all though grade school and they always did everything together. I have never seen the two of them fight, which I guess is a really good thing. In my opinion best friends should not fight or talk behind each other's backs, but we are human, so I just figure that gives me the right to do it. So as far as talking shit goes, I'd choose Maddie over Brooke any day. Brooke is way too anal; everything always has to be perfect, perfect, perfect. It drives me crazy if one corner of my bed is not made to her exact liking then she will fix it repeatedly until it passes her rigorous inspection.

Our next pair of wonderful girls are Stacey and Isabella. Both of them are downright gorgeous, both of them could have been models if they hadn't joined in with me. Isabella, like Brooke, was a dancer and really good at it too. She was mostly known for her brilliant red hair, and could be easily found anywhere in a crowd. What made her well known (other than her shoulder length, perfect waves, model-like hair) was that she had a tattoo of a ballet dancer that covered her entire back and seemed to move as she moved. It was almost as if the dancer in her back came to life as she moved around. The muscles in her back caused it to dance and flex almost mimicking her movements. I have to admit, it was pretty damn cool looking. Now Stacey was the skinniest girl in our entire group. I never went shopping with her because it made me feel very self-conscious, but if I had to go and pick something out for her it would be extra small and size zero, that's my guess. She danced because Isabella danced, she dyed her hair because Isabella did, and she does everything Isabella does. If I had to choose between the two of them, hands down it would be Stacey. Isabella always has to have her way and if she doesn't she throws the biggest fits. She is the second biggest drama queen I have ever known.

Last, but I'd like to think not least, we have me and Em. Emily and I have known each other since before we can even remember, but never really talked until we had this one class together. And of course, like most best friends we have our arguments and I get mad at her a lot. She tends to tell her opinion without thinking about how the other person will feel, and it definitely hurts sometimes. Also, I don't know how it happens this way, but if I meet a guy and happen to introduce him to her, he stops talking to me, every time! Whatever, we are supposed to be best friends, so I'll just keep it to myself. Em is very well known for her big boobs and the amazing sex, which is my guess as to why my guys go for her. Ever since I got my license, I have been driving her everywhere. Her birthday is only two weeks after mine, but her step-monster wouldn't let her get hers, I'm not really sure why, every time I ask I get a totally different answer so I stopped asking. It gets old, for those of us who do drive, to drive so far out of our ways just to get her. Sometimes I wonder if it would be better if she were one of the first to go. Emily by far is the biggest drama queen in the world. She will go as far as not talking to me for a week or more because of something so little and stupid that she over reacted on and kept to herself. The worst thing about her that bothers me is that she is always threatening to kill herself. We all know it's just for the attention, but she won't have my respect until she actually does it.

You will notice I do a lot of complaining about Em, and you can ask almost any of the other girls about her and they will all tell you that she is such a good person. Well that's only because they don't know her all that well, but I do. You will probably ask yourself, why am I still friends with her if all this stuff is true? Why the fuck do I put up with it all? Well I ask myself that every day, and I don't honestly know why. Stacey has told me that I am her hero because of all the shit I put up with and never say a word about it. If Em weren't around, I know that my best friend would probably be Stacey. In fact some days I wish that's who it was, but then again she has her moments too. Stacey is the most unreliable one of everyone. Hell would freeze over before she showed up on time or even early, and if she actually kept some of the plans she made, the world might cease to rotate. So to sum everything up, no one is perfect; some people just make it more noticeable that they aren't.

I do have a few friends outside of my group; cult is something you might call it, if that's what you are thinking about all this. And if that's the fact, then maybe you need to stop reading this right now because I wouldn't want to impose anything on you that might harm your innocent mind. Whatever, I don't have time to waste on you; as I was saying before, I have just a couple people outside my group who I rely on to keep my secrets and provide advice when I need it. First I have April, older, has more education under her belt and is a psychology major in college, boy do I need her help. Shut up, I don't need your two cents. Anyway, April likes to take the safe way; she is cautious and likes to ensure that everything she does is perfect and done the right way. Jamie on the other hand is my logical friend, she looks at things from outside the box, so sometimes it's the safe way and sometimes it's the practical way. She comes in very useful on occasion. Taylor would be considered the devil side of my conscious to April's angel side. She is not afraid to get dirty or get hurt, and I like that quality in a human, so she is one that I keep close. The last of my outside friends are Alexa and Amber. They are sisters and a mix of the other three. They are probably the only people who know just exactly what to say to make me smile even when I don't want to.

So I think I have covered everyone important, a few of my girls have boys and most of them have boy problems, but that's not very important, so I won't go into any more details about them. Boys are just a distraction, something to defer us from our paths in life. Love is overrated and just causes so much pain, that it's not even worth it. Love is like giving someone the power to destroy you, but trusting them enough not to, and since we are all human; trust is not in our vocabulary. Don't give me that look, have you ever told your best friend something, and a week later another friend comes to you and confronts you about it? You know for a fact that you didn't tell that person, but somehow everyone knows. Try having that happen to you several times and see how much you trust that person, see how much you tell them after that. Thank you Em for making me realize this. I just wonder how many other secrets of mine you told the others. Another strike against you.

Just a moment ago my sister came to my door and rudely interrupted my thoughts.

"Hey Kris, are you in there?" All I could think was what in the world? She never goes out of her way to talk to me and I don't go out of mine either.

I walked to my door and opened it, just barely and sticking my head out of the thin crack, "what?"

She just stood there staring at me; I guess I looked just as different as the other girls. "I heard that one of your friends died the other day, and I wanted to say that I'm sorry and was wondering if you needed anyone to talk to."

Geeze, is the weather going funny or is it just me? It was probably the longest conversation we've had in years. "Nah, I'm fine. I'm just relaxing right now, taking it all in."

She looked almost as surprised as I felt inside; I really was being nice to her. Maybe death is better than I thought; then again, maybe it makes me soft. "Okay, well I was just checking." She turned to walk away and then stopped and turned back to me, "If you don't mind me asking, how did she die?"

What an odd question, though I guess her parents would want to keep it out of the papers, "she drowned in the swimming pool at her house, it was a suicide." I could tell that made her think. Her eyes drifted to another place as she thought about what I had said. I could see a thin line of sweat bead on her brow as the reality of the event really hit her. The little wheels in her head were probably working overtime just to process what I had said, but she walked away and didn't ask anything more, smart kid. I suppose it would be hard to understand how a girl could kill herself in her own swimming pool, but somehow Ashlyn managed it.

Thinking back, I don't think I told you my name. I'm Kristen aka Kris. How could I introduce all those other girls and totally forget about myself? I'm the most important person! Yes, I'm full of myself and I love it. According to Maddie I have "the-world-revolves-around-me-syndrome." *Stands up and spins around in a circle. * You probably didn't understand that little part, but that's because it's an inside joke, and if you know what I meant, then congratulations to you, you're smarter than I thought.

Now I need to decide what to wear tonight. I guess I'll just wear the usual, jeans, tank top and sneakers. Best outfit ever, don't you agree? Unlike during some of our other acts of vandalism, we don't have to disguise ourselves because the cameras in our school are fake; the only place in our entire school that has an alarm to protect it is the library. God forbid if someone steals one of the precious books, to hell with all the computers and laptops, save the books. I'm so glad I'm finally graduating, that school is so full of bullshit. The assistant principal used to be a math teacher and somehow moved up to be assistant principal; he's practically a Nazi! This is the main reason I'm glad that we graduate in exactly one month. I can't wait to see the drama when we expose all the affairs that are going on in our school. Get this: the nurse is wife to the principal. The nurse is sleeping with the assistant principal and the principal is sleeping with the new gym teacher. That school is going down!

Anyway, yes I do like that word: anyway. So anyway, the girls should be here soon and we can head over to the school and get to work. I tend to lose track of time when I write, but I guess all great masterminds have that problem too. Actually, looking at the clock, they are late. Well, I guess so much for reliability.

I suppose this means I can keep writing. Yippee! Yes, that was meant to sound sarcastic. So I've been thinking about my death. Two ways I do not want to die: drowning and burning to death. I seriously don't know how Ashlyn got the guts to stay underwater long enough to drown herself, that girl had balls. I do know that I want to go out in a cool way, just exactly how is the question. Well I do have a few months left to think about it, to perfect it.

Where in the world are these girls? It's not like we have all night! I have a guess as to where they are. They probably had to drive somewhere else to pick somebody else up. It gets old having to do that all the time. Though I guess you wouldn't know, since you never had to do it.

And the doorbell rings. Isn't it weird how you think about someone or talk about them and it could be a few minutes or even a few hours and you see the person you were talking about. I'm not sure if that's totally awesome or really creepy.

Well it's time to have some fun. I will let you know how it went when I get back.

May 3rd

Success! We got in, we got out, no one saw us. That was probably the easiest "job" we had ever done. It was indoor, so we didn't have to watch our backs for cops passing by, the job was perfect and I would do everything again in a heartbeat. So we got in the auditorium and just spray-painted the shit out of everything! We wrote messages to our hated teachers and switched the senior slideshow disc from pictures of our graduating class to video of different teachers messing around with each other. I guarantee this will be a night to remember. I know I will never forget it.

Alicia is driving me crazy. She's the next to go and she's asking for everyone's opinion of what to do. Can she just be a little creative for once in her life? Is it too hard to ask for her to think for herself?

And when she's not busy bugging everyone about how to do it, she's reading her precious Bible. She told Stacey, who told me, that she's afraid she's going to hell for this. Well, there is a big chance of that, but if she was so afraid of it before she shouldn't have committed. She is way too religious for me. I'm not saying don't have a religion. Just don't flaunt it or shove it in everyone's face. That is one thing I cannot stand. I have no problem with the fact that she goes to church, and I have no problem with who she worships, it's just how that bothers me. I don't care that she wants to pray before every meal, but for her to ask the rest of us to either be silent or join in her prayer is ludicrous. She's constantly reading the Bible and tries to get us to read it too. If I was really all that interested then I would read up on it for myself, but since I'm not then the subject should be dropped and left alone.

See I'm dropping the subject. It's dropped. Gone now. All better.

Though, if I do see her with that book in her hands again I just might punch her in the face. Now it's dropped.

So how about this weather? All it's been doing is raining! What would Alicia say? Maybe the angels are here to wash away all of our sins! Yeah, okay. Anyway, this totally ruins our plans. Our next task was to go to the park and mess up anything that the school's parent committee had set up ahead of time, and maybe we could vandalize some of the buildings around there too. Just the usual stuff. But unfortunately the rain prevents us from doing that. Which probably means that the carnival will start off fine, but who says that it will end okay? I'll just have to come up with something else.

Oh yes, the carnival. Every year before graduation the town gets together and throws this big carnival at the park. It's our senior picnic, but we don't have to do any work, all we have to do is show up and have fun. Well, fun for some is not so much fun for others. Fun for me would be leeches in the dunking booth, but that would not be much fun for the person who gets dunked. Fun for someone . . . say prissy little Leah Eriksson, head cheerleader and top bimbo of our class, would be the kissing booth. To me that is just hell.

Looking at that girl just makes me want to gag. She is definitely not pretty, but she wears the most revealing clothes and always has on so much make up. When you can see the layers of foundation and they are peeling off your face, that is way too much make up. It's all the rage right now. Though you mostly see it in the underclassman, usually by the time they become seniors they realize how bad it looks, but then there's people like Leah.

What makes it even worse is who her boyfriend is. Caleb Morgan. It's a stereotypical relationship: head cheerleader dates head football player. Dumbest girl in school dates dumbest boy in school. Isn't that how it is in all the movies? Yeah, I just gagged again. Something that does surprise me about her is that she doesn't really have a band of faithful followers. I mean the other cheerleaders are pleasant to her, but I never see them hang out. Leah is usually attached at the hip to her precious Caleb or sitting alone playing with her hair and makeup and talking on the cell phone. I guess her life isn't so movie perfect as it seems on first glance.

This weather is driving me crazy! It's like it never stops raining. All I do is sit inside and write, drink and smoke. But, on second thought, it's not so bad. I could be slaving away at a crummy part time job or entertaining my mother's fake friends.

Just think, if I wasn't writing, you wouldn't be learning. You'd be sitting there bored, or reading another pointless book or watching a dumb movie. Now you realize how shitty your life is because you're sitting there reading about my shitty life and now realizing how shitty your life truly is.

Also, I'm glad you can put up with my attention slip ups. I hesitate to say my "A.D.D." because I was not diagnosed with it, but I got something. If I didn't you would be bored stiff reading this. Here how about this:

Q: How many kids with A.D.D. does it take to change a light bulb?

Don't you know the answer to this? Okay I'll tell you.

A: Wanna ride bikes?

Get it? Isn't that great? I love that joke! I don't know who came up with it first, but he or she is my hero!

Back on topic. Shouldn't I be thinking dark thoughts? I must be evil since I came up with this crazy death thing. Well if you are thinking that, then I say it again. Stop reading now. Wait, no don't stop. Finish reading what I have to say and if you still disagree, share this with someone else. Let it corrupt their mind too. Aren't I just evil?

I guess since I'm staying in tonight this means TV dinner time! Whoever invented those is a god. I can't even call them my hero because they deserve to be worshiped for what they made. The best advice I can give for eating TV dinners is don't look. If you do you will get grossed out and not be able to keep it down. Seriously, take a good long look at one sometime, and after you have stared at it come and tell me you are still going to eat it. I guaran-damn-tee you can't. But they are so easy to make that I will never stop eating them and you shouldn't either.

Father at work, mother in family room, sister presumably in her own room, no one to interfere with the making and eating of said nasty meal, just makes my night better.

Breaking into the liquor cabinet doesn't sound so bad either; let's just say I've become an expert at it. Two little screws and all the happiness inside is mine. I used to fill the empty bottles up with similar colored liquids such as water and tea, but that got annoying because sometimes I would forget I emptied the bottle and go to mix a rum and coke and end up with coke and tea, not a good combination. So after I did that a few times I just threw the empties away. Lucky for me someone replaces them, and even luckier for me is mom used to drink a lot but cut back, so I just make up for her. Far as I know she thinks dad drank it and dad thinks she drank it, works for me, because it means when I throw a bottle away and one of them see it, it gets replaced, so I'm always fully stocked.

Here's another topic for you to digest, notice I said throw away a bottle, not recycle. I don't understand the point of it, putting one glass or plastic container separate from all other trash so it can be crushed down and remade and reused. Yuck, I don't want to use something that is made of other people's trash and I'm sure they don't want to use mine. It's more work to carry out two containers on trash day than it is one, like that extra work really does anything anyway. It's not going to stop global warming or cut down on pollution. Nothing can do that except for maybe no more cars, electric, smoke, waste, carbon dioxide, shit like that. So take all life forms off Earth and it will be saved! Yeah, exactly, that's not going to happen so quit worrying about it and just give up.

I guess I didn't really end anywhere the other day; I just stopped. That's my attention span for you!

I have spent the better parts of the past four days drunk off my ass scheming and plotting. Wondering where I was? Okay fine, I'll tell you. I was at Taylor's house. See since I was bummed about not being able to wreck our senior picnic she decided to console me and help me come up with a new plan. Unfortunately, I can't really read my own drunken handwriting or understand the little pictures. So I guess it was kind of pointless. But at least I had fun. Of all the people I talk to, she is one of the best. She knows exactly what things (legal and illegal) to do to have some crazy fun when you're drunk. I can't even tell you how many people's mail boxes we destroyed, and my poor aluminum bat has quite a few dents and scratches; actually so does her car from the many times we missed and smashed the sides. Her dad saw the car and just laughed, I was sure he'd yell. I guess he's just cool like that, I wish my parents were like her's; they are always there for her and mostly let her do what she wants. Though that "mostly" word is what makes me glad I don't have her parents, I like being able to do what I want, when I want.

So, seeing as I can't understand my new wreckage plan, we are going to stick with the old plan. I know we are cutting it really close, since the carnival starts tomorrow, but tonight is the night we go to the park; you know what I mean. Everyone is meeting here around eight-ish, well at least everyone is supposed to, but I decided not to pick up dear Emily. That means either someone else has to, she finds her own way, or she just doesn't come, end of story. I'm sick of doing it, so I'll take the day off; I think I've earned it.

I know I can be very mean sometimes, but that's what life has taught me. It has always been mean to me, so to survive I have to be mean right back. And I would love to continue with that thought, but I just heard the front door open and close which means that at least one of the girls is here. None of them have permission to walk right in, but they do it anyway. Maybe we should start locking that door, because they only ring the doorbell when it's locked, and since it rarely is, they are constantly walking in and out.

Speaking of the devil, its Emily, and Alicia. They do live pretty damn close to each other but then Alicia always finds these excuses why she can't drive people. Usually those excuses begin with her mom, and then I say, "Fuck your mom, you are a grown ass woman and she's still telling you what to do." Of all the girls, Alicia belongs the least. Yeah, she looks the part, but she still talks to her parents and probably loves them for all I know. Also I would think that a churchgoer is the last person to belong here. Taylor would have been a better person for the part, but she told me that she already has plans of her own. I'm curious to see what she's doing; hopefully it happens before it's my turn to go.

Emily is chattering nonstop about some guy she saw at the grocery store, and Alicia listens intently (she has never been kissed or even had a boyfriend, talk about sheltered). I just sit and stare at them, why enter a conversation when I hate guys with all my heart.

When you fall so deeply in love that it seems like nothing else matters but the one you are in love with, and then he dumps you for another fucking girl, tell me you won't hate guys. I got dumped for a skinnier, prettier girl, a goddamn red head! I'm definitely prejudiced about redheads now; in fact I down right hate them. I can't tell you how many weeks I spent crying over him. That's when I realized that guys are just not worth it; their sole purpose on this earth is to break girls' hearts. I never understood the meaning to the song called "Headlights" by The Classic Crime, one line in it says, "Love is empty, love is cruel, love it blindly breaks the rules." After he dumped me, I realized the full meaning of those words; and realized love sucks.

Lost in my own little world, I didn't realize Alicia was talking to me, ". . . dunking booth, food stands, the stage, and a bunch of rides." Oh, I see, she's talking about all the things that are set up at that carnival/picnic thing. I just nod, that way I don't say anything wrong and she will never know that I wasn't paying attention.

I hear the door downstairs open and close again and soon enough Madison, Brooke and Isabella walk into my room. Wrapped up in their own conversation, I go back to ignoring all of them. All we have to do is wait for Stacey yet, typical. She is the least reliable out of all them. Always late or even sometimes never even showing up, she never returns phone calls and if you leave a voice message she doesn't even listen to it. If you have ever dealt with someone like her before you know what I mean and you know how frustrating it can be. Next time I call her and she doesn't call me back, I'm going to take her phone and jam it in her eye. That'll teach her to be stupid. Again I hear the door; well I'll be damned, only ten minutes late.

My bedroom door slams open and she rushes in looking half crazy. "Shepard's looking for you." They all look at me waiting for an explanation, but I smile and shrug.

"What did you do this time?" asked Emily.

I couldn't help it, I had to laugh. Now they're getting worried. No one messes with Pat Shepard; he's the guy who everyone is afraid of in our school. He's like 21 and a senior in high school, that's what you get for fucking around for three years.

They're waiting for me to give an answer, casually I say, "Well, I slashed his tires, spray painted all the windows black and carved some stuff into the doors." The looks on their faces are just priceless. "Are you crazy? He will kill you, especially since you messed with his Mustang," is what Isabella practically screamed.

"I was bored." This should be a Master Card commercial:

Spray paint: $12
Kitchen Knife: $8
The look on your friends' faces when they realize
you are going to be murdered: PRICELESS

Again, me not paying attention to them and being lost in my own little world, I'm missing out on their conversations. One of them asked, "How exactly does Shepard know it's you?"

I give them one of my innocent looks and say. "I carved my name into his hood so everyone who saw it would know it was me." That brought out another outburst of shock from them. What can I say; I'm just good like that.

"Okay everybody shut up. Our carnival is tomorrow, so we have to get as much destruction done tonight as possible. I'd suggest getting into the food stands and switching ingredients, or cutting small holes in the balloons so they can't blow them up, or think of something clever to do to the rides. Do whatever you want, just make sure not everything is obvious. We want them to have some surprises."

Leave it to Alicia to say, "Just be careful with what you do, we don't want anyone getting hurt tomorrow."

I'm going to be totally honest, I don't really care if people get hurt, serves them right if they do. I hadn't actually planned to do something where people might get hurt, but accidents do happen.

Time to leave, who knows if I will be back tonight or not, so until next time then.

May 10th

I have made it back alive from several days filled with fun, chaos, and pain.

To begin, the carnival was a complete crazy mess, after two hours of everything going wrong and none of the equipment working, the parents and other volunteers who had set everything up canceled it and sent everyone home. I'm not sure if the police or parents suspect anyone yet. That covers the fun part.

Next is chaos, someone; could have been one of my girls or maybe someone I don't even know; opened several gates to pastures where cows, goats and sheep were. Which means that they all got out and into the road, which created problems with driving because the animals wouldn't move. It took a group of volunteers more than a day to collect all the livestock and get them back to their proper owners.

And last but not least, the pain part. Let's just say Shepard found me and I will never ever touch his car again. The entire time I was getting beat up all I could think about was maybe he will finish me off and I won't have to worry about me not being able to do it myself. Isn't that just pathetic? Sometimes I make myself sick. Hey, whatever happened to the unwritten rule of guys can't hit girls?

I think someone, somewhere, someday should write a book of the unwritten rules of life, and then they wouldn't be unwritten anymore and everyone would know what they were and no one could break them . . . like guys can't beat up girls and people in a school band are called band geeks. See what I mean? I'm sure if I really thought about it I could come up with a big list of unwritten rules that should be written down.

May 15th

I had to have a nice long chat with the girls today. Last night we went out to the movies and to the dinner afterwards and Isabella and Stacey were messing around and laughing and having fun. Well the first of my rules is that in public, you do not show people your feelings and emotions. It's just not done. The best way to prevent from people going out of their way to talk to you is to put on a front and look mean. I made it clear to all of them, but it seemed like they needed a reminder. I've been letting them do pretty much what they want when I should be strict and a bitch. It's so much easier when the people under you fear you, then there is no question of authority. We all had a nice long chat today, and I explained that there would be no displays of anything in public other than a neutral expression. I focused most of my attention on Stacey because at one point last night she had stood up on her booth and began to throw jelly packets all over the dinner. It would have been fine if she had kept a straight face but no, she laughed and carried on.

You could say that I'm a bitch, maybe I am. But no one is going to succeed or get anywhere in the world without discipline.

My main reason for keeping them from appearing to be having fun is the possibility that they catch someone's eye (a boy) and he becomes interested and pursues her and she falls for it, which means that all my plans are ruined and I have to go on living. No boy in their right mind is going to be attracted to a girl who sits straight-faced and silent while in the company of her friends. He will assume she is boring or just a plain old bitch and won't even try to go after her. That way I don't have to kill him just so she kills herself. It just makes my life a whole lot easier.

May 20th

I have come to the realization that I hate myself. I hate the way I look. Who in this day and age wears a size 6 jean? No one that's who. I'm fat and ugly. Don't argue with me because you know it's true.

May 30th

After starving myself for a week and then barely eating for the past three days, I've gained two pounds! It's pathetic! I'm pathetic! How does Stacey stay so skinny? She eats all the time and yet is skinny as a twig. I hate it and I hate her. Stupid bitch all skinny and to top it off now she's all giddy because she has a stupid boyfriend. Just the thing I was hoping wouldn't happen! He saw her the night she carried on at the diner and fell for her right away. Then she fell for his stupid love songs and poems and shit. It's so cheesy, who falls for that kind of thing anymore? There's only one thing for me to do now . . . Get rid of him.

The "most important day of my life so far" (as our principal had told us) is coming up in a day and I'm planning murder. Just great.

Graduation today, you should have been there, it was great. First the look on the principal's face when he found out his wife (the school nurse) was sleeping with the assistant principal and then the look on her face when she found out he was cheating on her with the gym teacher; it was priceless! Some of the shit we wrote to and about our teachers made some of them walk out of the auditorium. The senior slide show was just the disaster we had planned, pictures of different teachers making out in back corners and a few selective videos (practically pornography) of the tenth grade English teacher fucking first the gym teacher, then the ninth grade math teacher, then the twelfth grade physics teacher, and last his own student teacher, I guess it's safe to say that he got around.

By the time all that had happened the commencement speaker had left and our superintendent had nearly all the faculty, including the principal and assistant principal, removed. Watching her we all had to laugh, she was so short she couldn't see over the podium, and her ass was so big she had a hard time getting out of the chair. For nearly twenty minutes she apologized to all the families and friends in the auditorium. I thought for a minute there that she might cancel graduation all together, but instead she picked up the name sheets and stated, "Might as well get this over with." So she went through the alphabet, calling our names one by one. Of my girls it went Brooke then Madison, me,

Isabella, Emily and Stacey, then she announced Alicia's name, but she wasn't there. I had totally forgotten that today was her day! I saw her parents and all three of her brothers in the audience, they looked around all confused but our superintendent moved on. I felt ridiculous as I made eye contact with Emily who mouthed "I totally forgot." I guess I wasn't the only one.

Right at the end, when everyone's name had been called, there were still two diplomas left. One I knew was Alicia's, the other I couldn't figure out because everyone else had walked when their name was called. Again she began talking, "A little over a month ago our school lost a valuable member, this class lost a good friend, so today we present her diploma to her parents. Will the parents of Ashlyn Cowell please come up here?" Oh, okay well that explains it, her mom walked up all teary-eyed and her father walked like he had a stick in his ass. After that our oh-so-wonderful valedictorian led us in the moving of the tassel. Then it was over. Parents hugging their kids and taking pictures. Isabella, Stacey, and I all stood alone in the back, of course our parents didn't show up, but we did have to wait for the others while their parents hugged and kissed them, but looking at their faces I could tell they weren't enjoying it. When they could sneak away they did and we all slipped out the back door. I heard Stacey and Brooke mumbling to themselves, but I couldn't make out exactly what. Brooke suddenly bursts out, "I can't believe I forgot! I didn't get to say goodbye or anything!" The other girls nodded in agreement, but I wasn't concerned about not getting to say goodbye. I was just surprised I had forgotten, it's not like me to forget about a death.

I was pretty sure they wanted to do something to celebrate graduation, but that happy, gay shit wasn't my cup of tea. Instead I pulled off the ridiculous gown and hat we had to wear, pulled out my lighter from my pocket, and set them on fire, to hell with that shit. I walked away in silence and left them there to argue over who would take who home.

So I've been home for a little over an hour now and have heard nothing from no one about Alicia. I bet the little shit didn't even do it. Figures ruin my plans; make my job harder, murder is so much more difficult than suicide. I guess I'll just have to wait until tomorrow and see if she did or not.

June 3rd

I'll be damned; the little shit proved me wrong! Killed herself dead she did. Found out from her oldest brother last night. Fact #1: He is AMAZING in bed! Wow. Fact #2: Her parents found her that night in the barn at their place . . . crazy bitch hung herself! Funny thing is; she didn't even tie the knot right! A right knot will break the neck and kill instantly; a wrong knot leads to death by strangulation. Let's just say it was a wrong knot that killed her. What a dumbass.

But back to her brother, never before has any boy left me weak afterwards. If I could do it again I would, many times over and over again. It probably only lasted ten minutes, but it felt like an hour, it was that good.

You know what I hate about high school? The drama. And even though I've only been graduated a whole three days, I've realized that the stupid drama crap follows you right out and where ever you go. I just got an email from Emily who thinks Isabella hates her, well she does, but I'm not telling her that. To be honest, I'm not sure who really does like Emily, she's moody and very hormonal, we all put up with her, and in her presence we are pleasant, but as soon as she's out of sight, everyone is talking shit on her. I can't truly say I talk shit, because I hardly talk, but I can think it. And like I said before, it's safer to not tell anyone what you really think because then within a few days everyone knows. Some friends I have.

Oh, and I almost forgot! You remember Stacey's boyfriend? Well he disappeared the day after graduation. Well technically he only disappeared for a few hours and then his parents found him all beat up and nearly dead in their driveway. Till the ambulance got there and he got to the hospital, he was dead; bled to death or drowned when his ribs punctured his lungs; I've heard both rumors. I'm proud of myself for that one, didn't even have to lay one hand on him. Let's just say that a friend of a friend owed me a favor and now their debt is resolved. Here's something to remember; always keep a few people around who owe you a big favor, you never know when something will turn up and you really need them to do your dirty work.

June 5th

Got myself a job today. Just something to do to pass the time until summer's over, and I have to go to college. It's not like I need the money, I just don't want to spend time with the remnants of my group.

I bet you're curious now. Wondering who would ever hire me, or is there really a place on earth I would ever consider working. Well there is. It's a salon located in the middle of our only shopping center in town, and being the only place like it within a 30 minute driving range, it's very popular and always packed, which is where I come in. I am a desk receptionist. What I do is answer the phone and write people in our calendar, schedule their appointments for hair, nails, waxing, things like that. It's a boring job where I have to pretend to be pleasant, but it's easy money.

My first day is tomorrow and I'm not really excited. Maybe I should practice a greeting and get really good at it; it wouldn't be very good if I got fired for bitching at a customer on the first day.

June 6th

Talk about an interesting day. I spent all morning on the phone, making appointments. Then, right around noon, exactly when my boss (Carrie) said it would, there were no calls. She told me that from noon on it would be slow, so my only other task was to wait for the mail carrier and separate each of the stylists' mail for them and put it in separate bins behind the counter.

Well, the mailman is really a mail kid. He's my age. Anyway, he strolls in like he owns the place, greets the ladies there and comes up to my counter. Soon as he sees me his mouth falls wide open, and he drops the huge stack of mail he's holding.

"Nick!" Carrie had shouted.

He just blushed and picked all the mail up. After he set it on the counter he practically ran out the door.

Carrie explained that he was her nephew and was working for the mail office as a summer job, which means I'll be stuck seeing him every day all summer. Yippee for me.

June 7th

5 months and 23 days left

Nick came in the salon three times today, claiming each time that he had forgotten a letter for one of the girls. Carrie just laughed, and he just blushed and left.

"I think he likes you," she said after the third time.

"I hope not, who wants to date someone with a dirty mop on his head?"

At that she laughed, "He has his own style my Nick."

Yeah, ripped jeans, a dirty t-shirt, hair too long and very dirty looking. I guess it would be a style okay for bums. Bums, HA! I crack myself up.

June 8th

Rumor has it that I am the longest lasting employee at the salon. I mean there are stylists and other people who are there every day, but they are all close friends with Carrie and aren't considered employees. I've only worked there for three days and I'm being told that I'm the best person she has ever hired and the one who has made it the longest. Does that give me the right to brag?

Daniel, the gayest of gay men who works there told me that the last girl Carrie only hired to see how mean of a boss she could be till the girl quit. Supposedly she only lasted two hours. It makes me feel good about myself; at my last two jobs I busted my ass and never even got noticed. You might go home and complain how tired you are, but you will never know the true meaning of tired. How about working an eight hour shift, leave to work a different job for four hours and then go back to the first job and work another six hours; then tell me you are tired; anything else is just lazy.

Speaking of lazy, Emily is laying on my bed bitching and complaining about who knows what. She showed up here soon after I got off work, and she hasn't moved since. All I know is that she was crying for like an hour and then went off on some rant and is now talking normally but I'm still not listening. She's not worth it. Damn it where's Isabella when I need her? I love to watch the two of them together because Isabella hates Emily, but Emily is too damn dumb to know it, so she gets all buddy

buddy and I get to laugh as Isabella pretends to kill Emily behind her back. There is one day I will never forget. The first day in over a year that Isabella actually talked nicely to Emily, and Emily thought it was the greatest thing in the world, so she starts calling Isabella and thinks they are the bestest friends ever, and then Isabella punches her; right in her fat face. I love it, best memory of the two of them.

Insert a breath of relief; it just got silent in here. I think she is finally done with her pointless talking. But I should have known it, she wants Taco Bell. She burned off so many calories talking that she needs to eat before she dies of starvation, god forbid she loses a few pounds.

I will be back another time or another day; maybe I will be less one Emily. I could just dump her body in the construction site along the highway after she feeds herself. Oh wait, that would ruin everything, I'll just have to deal with her a little longer.

After all I was told the other day about being the longest lasting employee at the salon; I'm considering quitting my job. Don't get me wrong, I love the job, it's a great job, it's easy as shit and Carrie is a cool boss. Like I said before, it's not like I need the money, it was just something to keep me occupied over summer. It's just that stupid kid, that boy who visits at least 3 times a day. Every time he comes in he stares at me for a couple minutes and then tries to talk to me about the most random shit that I could care less about. He is driving me crazy and Carrie tells him to leave all the time but he doesn't take her seriously because they are family.

Today when he was in I told him that I could just punch him and then he wouldn't be able to stare at me anymore. It didn't faze him one bit. Instead he sat on a stool on the other side of the counter from me and began talking about his friends and the crazy things they do. He was bragging that they beat this kid up so bad he ended up in the hospital. Obviously, I wasn't impressed, in a roundabout way I was involved in nine deaths and counting . . . he had nothing on me.

He also asked me out. I said hell no and walked outside for a cigarette. Of course he followed me, so I blew my smoke in his directions and tapped my ashes on his foot, but he didn't take the hint . . . what a dumbass. For the rest of the time I had to work he followed me like a damn puppy dog wanting me to take him home. Let's just say that that will never happen.

Now that I think about it, I will quit. I won't ever have to see him again and on the plus side, then I won't have to do anything anymore. I can go back to being my lazy bum self. I like that idea.

June 14th

Carrie wasn't the happiest person when I talked to her yesterday at work. I know now that she really does like me a lot because she practically begged me to stay. She offered me a raise and more hours if I wanted them. She even said she would kill her nephew for me if I would stay, so I told her that if he were six feet underground I would come back in a heartbeat. Of course, I know she won't kill him, but I would love to.

Well, that job was short lived; now I can sleep all day and night and not have to do a single thing.

This is the life.

June 17th

I got a job at the dollar store in town today. No stupid boy to bother me either.

I know, you are probably wondering what could have come over me to get a job this quick. I mean I did just quit my other one only four days ago. One word: Emily.

She is there all the time. Always invading my life and stealing my shit. I'm sick of it, so if I'm not home, she won't be there either. And now she really has nothing to do because she used to work at the same store, but they fired her so they could hire me. What can I say, everyone knows I'm better than her, she just doesn't realize it yet, one day she will see the light.

This will be an even easier job, all I do is stand around all day and ring register. I have a feeling I will like this job a lot more because both Alexa and Amber work there and they just hang out all day, so if there is another cashier on then I can sit and smoke all day with them. No one has a better job than me.

June 18th

So you remember that yesterday I said, "one day she will see the light?" Well, she saw the light today.

When I got home from work she was sitting here waiting for me. First, I got accused of stealing her job . . . which I did. Then she accused me of stealing her friends. It's not my fault they like me more than her. Then supposedly I ruined her life and she regrets ever being my friend.

None of what she says bothers me because I just don't care.

My reply to her is, "Fine. Then leave."

She definitely got confused at this. I bet she expected me to yell or cry or something.

"I said leave. If I have stolen everything from you and ruined your life then there is nothing more I can do for you, and so I have no use for you anymore. You are dismissed." Now I sound like the army.

"What if I don't want to leave?" she asked with an attitude.

"Well, I could either punch you in the face so you leave, or let you stay. I don't feel like doing either because that requires me getting up, so just leave."

"Aren't we doing something tomorrow?"

"The girls and I are doing many things tomorrow, with, or without you. It's your choice. Just get out now."

I've never seen her leave my house so fast, it was amazing. Ungrateful son-of-a-whore, she would be nothing and nowhere without me. For three years now I have driven her everywhere, paid for her shit when she didn't have money and even sometimes when she did, and lied that she didn't. I'm the reason she has some of the friends she does. One of these days she will see that and come crawling back to me.

June 19th

Crawling.

Crawling.

Crawling.

She came crawling back today. I must be able to predict the future because that's two days in a row I did it. I guess she didn't want to lose the few friends she has left, especially me.

Today on the agenda is scoping out the new school. We are college girls now.

So supposedly like 50 years ago someone stole the eagle off the statue outside the main building, and just recently they found it stashed away in the ceiling in one of the dorms, so tonight I'm going to steal it again and stash it somewhere until someone else finds it.

The End.

Tricked you didn't I? You thought that was the end of this journal didn't you? Yeah, don't lie. Wouldn't that just be mean? You would never know what happened to me or the rest of the girls. Choose your own ending. I'm out of here.

June 21st

If I were writing a blog this is how it would go:

MADISON: Where did you get the perfume you are wearing?
ME: I stole it.
MADISON: You would.
ME: I did.
MADISON: You would.
ISABELLA: She did.
MADISON: She would.
ME: I did.

You do have to admit that it's a little funny.
I never said I had the brightest friends.

June 23rd

Even though today is only Tuesday I got drunk last night. I know, you must be thinking that I'm an alcoholic, but whatever I don't care. I had fun with my friends and that's all that matters.

I actually have to go to work today. Not like it's a bad thing, but I'm just not in the mood. I have a super hangover and everything seems to be pissing me off. I walked in the door and the rug was bunched up so the door wouldn't open all the way and that just made me furious, so I slammed the door shut and kicked the rug out of the way, then I tripped on the damn rug and got even more pissed, so I punched the wall going up the stairs and put a hole in it. Now my hand hurts and I'm really mad about it. It's fucking ridiculous! Damn it I need a drink.

I think I might call off sick. I'll say I have a doctor appointment, and they should let me off fine because Emily used to do it all the time and they never questioned her. I do have the fact that they actually like me, they're on my side, so I can get off even easier and do shit she never could have done. I like that kind of job.

Yep, I'm feeling sick. I have a fever and chills; I need to go to the hospital immediately. I'm calling in dead. Or, soon to be dead, or how about just sick. Sounds like a plan to me.

June 24th

What if you had a super power? How cool would that be? I'd love to be able to like walk through walls or fly or shoot fire from my hands.

If you are wondering where this came from, well I was watching a movie and it got me thinking. I would love to have a special something that puts me far apart from all other humans. Maybe I'd like to be invisible. I could sneak around, spy on people, steal things easier, it would be fun; you've got to admit it. Super strength would be good too because everyone would be afraid of me and then they'd leave me alone before I crush them to bits. I don't know, it's just a thought.

Here's another thought for you: did you ever think about your imagination? I know people have wild imaginations and some have no imagination at all. For those that do, I wonder if there are limitations to their imagination, like is there anything they can't think of and see it in their head. I have a pretty wild imagination, but I can't imagine any life for myself in the future. I see nothing for me, so I just wonder if that means my imagination is limited. Am I not as wild and awesome as everyone thinks I am? Am I a fake?

FUCK THAT! I'm perfect! It's the world that is wrong! It's every other human being on the earth that is imperfect because they aren't like me!

Okay, that's enough of that. End of this story. I'm done.

June 25th

I've been thinking: I do a lot of thinking. And I tell you all the time that I've been thinking. I think that maybe I think too much. Do you think so? Do you think I think too much?

I think about a lot of things that I don't tell you. Like all the mood swings I go through. Like the other day I was driving to work and a song that I've heard a million times came on the radio. I started singing along to it; well actually I yelled the words inside my car. It was one of those songs that the guitars are too loud and the singer screams the words into his microphone. Halfway through the first chorus I stopped singing and started crying. When I listened to the words closer they made me not just cry, but sob uncontrollably. I don't understand what came over me then, and it wasn't the first time that's happened to me. I can't listen to any of my favorite songs anymore, either I cry like a baby or get so pissed off I can hardly breathe. So, I've decided not to listen to music anymore. Maybe I need medication for my mood swings . . .

I also think that I'm in love with one of April's best friends, but he's married and loves his wife. If he didn't we'd have an affair for sure. I hope she's not catching on, she says we talk to each other too much. It's only like one email a day. That's not too much is it? I don't think so at least.

I think my mom is out to kill me. She had my sister bring me dinner to my room the other night, of course I didn't eat it, there's poison in that shit!

Alright well that's enough thinking for now; I think.

June 28th

So for the last three days I've been thinking about my thinking and then I was thinking about other things.

In two days Brooke dies. I wonder how Madison will deal because the two of them are inseparable. Maybe Madison will be so heartbroken she will kill herself early and then I can force Emily to die in August. That would give me a few months of an Emily free life, which I really need. I'm so sick of her; all she does is whine and complain about everything. If she is in the room all attention has to be focused on her or it's the end of the world, I swear! I believe (notice I didn't say think; shit, wait, I just did) that she makes herself cry for the attention and makes up health problems and family problems just so she can tell everyone who will listen. Then they will pity her and tell her all these lies just so she feels good about herself and will shut up. I'm sick of it and you would be too if you had to put up with her shit every single day . . .

On top of all that, and knowing very well she talks too much, she also says shit to make people like her more. She has been telling Alexa all these things that I either supposedly said or did, or like how she feels about me. For example, she said that when we drink together she feels like she has to stay sober so she can be my babysitter because I need one. That's a lie, I drink with so many other people and none of them think that. Another thing she said is that I'm really clingy and always attached to her hip. First off, she's the one who's always at my house, she calls me when she wants to do something, she calls me all the time for no reason, and since I'm the one who drives she has to go with me which usually means she would be attached to my hip. There's a whole lot of other things she's told people, but none of it's true, or if it is true, its blown so out of proportion that whoever is her victim and has to listen wouldn't believe her anyway. So pretty much, long story short: Emily is a fat, pimply, liar who wants to be me. I like that explanation, don't you?

July 1st

5 months left

Madison called me this morning, she told me that Brooke had called her right around midnight and was all scared and shit, what a pansy. I seem to have chosen the wrong group of girls for this; they are all scared or just not the type I would ever be friends with if I didn't have to.

I don't even quite remember how we ended up together. I know Emily, Stacey, and Isabella were all friends before and I had a class with Emily. I think at some point I mentioned to her that the class was so boring I could just kill myself and it just went on from there. I think Isabella knew Brooke through dance classes, which also brought in her sidekick, Maddie. Ashlyn and Emily were friends before, and Alicia, well she was just there. The first day that all eight of us got together to talk was probably the happiest day of my life. I felt like all my dreams were coming true. I had, for many years thought about how awesome it would be if a group of friends killed themselves to make a point, the point being that our lives suck.

April 2nd, two years ago, I will never forget that as the day we all first came to be together. I remember that everyone was so cheery except for me. Back then I was the outcast of the group, first thing on my list was to change that. For a whole year I went back and forth between Stacey and Emily, make one my best friend and then the other. After that I realized Emily was the lesser of the two evils, and so I cast Stacey aside.

It took a little over two years to get our plans assembled, but over that time the girls were changing, getting further away from their parents and becoming more like me. I think it was April 5th of this year that I'd had enough. We all talked about suicide, but had never gotten any further than cutting our wrists to bleed a little. On the night we were supposed to burn my house down, I called them and said there was a change of plans. Instead we met in my bedroom and talked. I told them that we needed to begin the real purpose of getting us together. The girls seemed excited about it at first, but when they realized someone would die in only a few weeks they sobered quickly. I explained that I would be the last to go because I wanted to make sure they all did it. Thinking back now, I'm pretty sure I was just afraid to die, but now I'm not afraid anymore. I do not fear death. Yay me!

We argued and compromised over what order we would go in and finally after several hours Ashlyn caved in and volunteered. I would have preferred Alicia, but she wanted to make sure we were really going to do it, so she wanted to go second. Then the rest just gave up fighting and decided when they would go. Everything was set, plans were made. On your mark, get set, go.

And that's the end of my walk down memory lane, just some dull thoughts to pass the time while I wait for a phone call to see if Brooke did it or not.

Can you even imagine what state of mind someone would have to be in to jump to their death? Standing at the highest height of a building, staring at the street below as the cars drive by, the wind that whips around the roof. I'm terrified just thinking about it. If you haven't guessed, I'm referring to Brooke. Her father owns a huge apartment complex that's nearly 15 stories tall. If the fall alone hadn't killed her then the 3 cars that ran her over after she landed would have. Her funeral will definitely not be open casket.

Emily is really pissing me off today, see we share the same cell phone plan, I had the plan first and then she never paid her bill with a different company, so the bill got to be like 600 bucks. Out of kindness I added her to mine and at first she paid me, but now she's not. It's not like she needs the money anyway. She has no other bills to pay and spends all her cash on fast food. That damn fat bitch doesn't need any more food, and then if she's not buying food, she's spending it on other shit she doesn't need like magazines and shoes. I'm really pissed at her so I think I'm just going to shut her phone off. That'll teach her to fuck with me. I thought it would be downright evil to cancel her phone on her birthday, but that's in mid-January and we won't be around then, so I'm going to the mall today with Alexa and Amber.

Alexa is a bit older than me, but Amber is my age. We graduated high school together, but we were never friends until recently. Amber has tons of parties and Alexa invites me, so that's how I met her.

And now I have to leave to go meet them, so I will continue later. Cheers.

Cheers, I must elaborate on that word. My one ex-boyfriend used to say that all the time and it made him sound so retarded, I would get mad every time he said it. Then I broke up with him and since we were in school together I would still run into him and ever since then when I heard him say, "cheers" I punched him. Eventually he learned not to say it.

Yesterday when Alexa, Amber, and I went to the mall we got stuck in the elevator. It was actually kind of fun, Amber was freaking out because we kept pressing buttons. I shut off Emily's phone and didn't tell her. So when she goes to call someone she will hear a message saying her phone is not capable to send or receive calls, I'm such a bitch.

Amber called me a little bit ago to tell me they are throwing a huge party tonight. It's not a special occasion or anything, but do we really need a reason to party? No, I didn't think so.

July 4th

I hesitate to say "happy" Independence Day because people around the country are celebrating the freedom well earned by our country's armies. See I'd rather celebrate all those people who died while fighting. I don't care which side they were fighting on, they died and death makes me happy, so I'll celebrate that.

My parents and sister are out at some picnic having fun doing their thing. I am preparing to go to April's house. Her husband got his hands on quite a bit of free alcohol, and he's invited everyone he knows over to have a party. I hear the word party and I'm there. Even though I'm not very big on socializing with lots of people, parties are the best place to learn all the interesting gossip and drama about different people. I don't care whether I know the person who the story is about or not, if other people are talking about one person, then whatever they are saying has to be some good juicy gossip, or else why would they waste their breath on telling everyone about it. I live, breathe, eat, and sleep gossip. Gossip is a healthy part of my daily nutritional routine. Plus, parties are the only place to get all you can drink, free alcohol and try the latest, greatest drugs that are making their way around schools.

Not to brag or anything, but I am the beer pong champion. None of the guys can beat me, they've tried. The thing I like most about these parties is that once I drink a little I can be my true self, I can let loose and have some fun; don't tell the other girls though.

I love Rice Krispies. It is the best cereal ever! I love that it's crunchy and soggy and doesn't have a fake taste. I could eat an entire box in one sitting. But not cocoa krispies, I like chocolate milk, and I like rice krispies, just not mixed. That's gross.

Another really tasty treat is to eat some sort of fruit snack and then smoke a cigarette, tastes so good. I don't think they make fruity cigarettes or I'd be all over that shit.

4 months and 25 days left

So, I've got this friend who was dating a girl, broke up with her after three weeks, went out with another girl right after that for three weeks, broke up with her and then dated a third girl right away. I mean like the day after they broke up he's got another girl friend. But that's not all, exactly two weeks after being with this girl he proposed. She said yes, but then four days later she broke up with him because she was scared. Then he begged for her back, and she took him back, so they dated for two more weeks, not engaged just dating and she broke up with him again because he had his first girlfriend that I mentioned come over to play video games. Again he begged and pleaded for her to take him back, and the crazy bitch did. Back to the dating, all they did was fight and she broke up with him again but then this time she wanted him back, I don't know why. After like three weeks he proposed again and she demanded she got to pick out her own ring. So they arranged to meet at the mall to pick one out, well she called him while he was driving there to say she wasn't coming, he should do it another day. So he turned around and while he was driving back home she called him and asked if he got one. He said no so she broke up with him. He turned around again, went to the mall and picked out a ring, bought it right then and there and left to go to her house to get her back and give her the ring. While he was driving to her house, they passed on the road and he called her and she said she was going to the mall to pick out her own ring. He told her that he got one and was on the way to give it to her and she broke up with him AGAIN because he wouldn't let her pick out her own. They both end up going to the mall so he can return the ring and let her pick out her own. When they got there she couldn't pick one out and got mad at him because it would have been better for him to surprise her with one, which he was trying to do in the first place. They finally agreed on a ring and went home. They spent one whole month together, fighting the entire time but not breaking up, and she goes crazy on his ass, being bi-polar and controlling his life. For three weeks she wouldn't give him sex so he fucked a fake vagina and he used a condom, but forgot to throw it away after, so she thought he cheated on her, so she broke up with him again. He explained it to her and she got madder because she said it was almost like cheating. They got back together a couple days later and then still continued to fight and fight. So finally he broke up with her, but since he's such a dumbass he went right back the next day and they go on as they were, just fucking miserable. Well last night his girlfriend/fiancée whatever was in a horrible accident, some crazy ass driver forced her car off the side of the road and down a nasty cliff and she died. This morning he got his ass royally handed to him and is unfortunately still living, for now.

Moral #1 of the story: Don't be a crazy ass motherfucker like her, and don't be someone who puts up with all that shit, it's not good for your health, you will die.

Moral #2 of the story: If you want something done right you better do it yourself. I said dead and only half of it was carried out; the other half is lying in a hospital bed just waiting for me to come along.

Maybe I should tell you that the guy that I was telling you about is my ex-boyfriend. I was the first girl he dated, and then he dumped me for that psycho bitch. I had her killed because she tortured him and made him miserable. Then I wanted him killed for two reasons: the entire time he was with her he told me everything that was going on and I had to suffer it too. The whole time I thought to myself how I would have been so much better for him and to him because I would be nothing like her and how he would be so happy with me. So I was miserable thinking about it all. The second reason was because he dumped me, no one dumps me; it's just not done. Now I'm going to change that old saying: Hurt me once, shame on you. Hurt me twice, shame on me. Hurt me three times . . . well I will fix it so you can't.

And that, ladies, is why you don't date, because you won't fall in love and then they can't break up with you and you won't get hurt. It's that simple. How many times must I say it?

Lucky me though, my guys did that hardest part, now all I have to do is finish it. Simple enough, a fall down the stairs should do it, seeing as his skull is so fragile right now. If not I'll come up with something else; I'm good at improvising.

I'm not telling you how I did it, but it's done, no more mean man.

The girl's funeral is today and I've decided to go to it. All I want to do is spit on her grave, fucking whore. You would hate her too if you were me.

Not tomorrow, but most likely the day after will be his funeral. Emily will probably go because she dated him a long time ago, but he dumped her because she's fat, so she never really got over him. I might go just so I can spit on him too.

Maybe while I'm there I can spit on Emily too, she disgusts me. I actually never noticed it before, until Isabella mentioned it. Emily wears clothes that are way too small for her. To put it nicely, she is a big girl and her clothes are made for little girls, so those nasty purple stretch marks are always showing, I never truly looked at her so I didn't notice, but Isabella pointed it out and now I can't stop staring. It's one of those things where you don't want to look, but you just can't help it.

Now you are probably mad at me for saying that, so I guess I should explain myself. I don't hate fat people, I don't have anything against them, hell I never said I was skinny, I just wish I was. The only person I have a problem with being fat is Emily. Some of my friends are skinny and some are not, but they are all the same, except for Emily.

I think it's just because she makes me so miserable. I just want to do something to her for revenge and this is my way. Plus, I just like to talk shit on her; so don't hate me because I hate her. If it helps you any, I'll tell you my weight. Or, maybe I won't because I'm too damn self-conscious. So yeah, just trust me, I'm not as perfect as I have led you to believe.

What the hell was I on yesterday? I can't believe I confessed one of my deepest, darkest secrets! I could just easily erase it all, but for some reason, I'm leaving it there, maybe it's so you can understand me a little better.

I'm in such weird moods lately, up and down, left and right, back and forth, I never know which way I'll be at any given moment. Just this morning I was joking around with April and then she said something to me, something I've gotten used to her saying, but for some reason I just got really mad and then had to come up with an excuse to leave. I didn't want to hurt her feelings, so I left, and five minutes later I had to pull my car over so I could sit there and scream. I pounded on my steering wheel and screamed my frustration. Two six-packs of beer and a pack of cigarettes later, I am calm.

There is this really hot guy that works in the liquor store down the street from where I work, and I know for a fact he deals in drugs. So the other night I left a note for him to give me a call because I'm looking for some pills. And just ten minutes ago he called, I pretty much told him that I think I'm bipolar and need some shit to take care of it. Unfortunately he doesn't have anything for me, so I just ordered some Vicodin or something like that, helps me to fall asleep better. Well, I have to go meet him so; I will talk to you later.

July 10th

Liquor store guy is definitely very hot. I don't even know his name, but who cares. As long as I can stare at him, I'm happy. He's actually really dumb and when he talks he sounds kind of slow, so I'm going to stare from a distance. The idiot couldn't even count the money I gave him, lucky for me because I was thirty bucks short, sucks for him.

So I got a cold from going out last night and it fucking sucks. My throat is all scratchy and I keep coughing. I can't even smoke a damn cigarette! My favorite part of getting sick though, is the cough syrup. I could drink that shit for hours. Put it in a damn sippy cup for me and I'll be the happiest person alive (or dead). Especially if it's cherry flavored, grape is good too. Death by cough syrup, now that's an idea.

This stuff actually makes me really tired, so I'm going back to bed. Fuck work.

That damn kid from the hair salon came into work today! I swear he knew I was working because he came right in grabbed the first thing he saw and headed for my line. I scanned people's items really slowly so that another cashier had to come up and ring backup, but the bastard stood through my extra-long line and refused to go anywhere else. When he handed me his money there was an extra piece of paper included. On it was his phone number. I made a big show of ripping it into tiny pieces and throwing it away. Luckily he left without bugging me anymore. God I thought I was finally rid of him!

This is like the salon all over again; he came in four separate times today! He'd always buy one thing and stand forever in my line and never say anything, just stare. My manager actually asked me about it because she noticed that I was always pissed off after he left. I just told her he was a stalker and I'd take care of him. She did inform me that if he kept doing it I could say something to her and she'd kick him out for harassing me. That suggestion didn't sound too bad, but I'd rather beat the shit out of him myself. It's more fun that way.

College begins September 1st but I got my schedule in the mail today. It came with a list of books I would need and other suggestions for things I might need in my classes. Like hell I'm going to waste my money on that shit. Even if I did go to class I would never read the books, so why waste the money? I mean I do have the extra cash to waste but I was thinking more along the line of a new cell phone or maybe even a laptop. I strongly dislike my desktop computer; I can't take it with me.

Here's another thing I hate: my hair. I have friends who can wake up in the morning, wash their hair and let it air dry and it will dry perfectly straight. Not mine. Mine dries in waves and curls, and it's so thick it takes forever to dry. The worst part is that when I wash, dry and straighten my hair it takes me nearly 3 hours! I do this almost every day! I'd get it chemically straightened but that would really kill my hair, so I'll just have to deal.

Speaking of dealing, I have to go meet Alexa and Amber so we can come up with a shopping list of alcoholic beverages we need for the weekend. Bye bye for now.

Soap operas are so fucking stupid. It's all crap about someone cheated on someone else with their best friend who is pregnant with her uncle's neighbor's cousin's baby, and in the end it turns out they are all related, or some shit like that. Oh yeah, and someone is always in the hospital in a coma. The *days of their lives* are spent in that *general hospital* and since they've only got *one life to live* they spend all their time with *all* their *[my] children*. Get my references?

Can you tell I was bored earlier? Yeah, I really was. I stole a TV from this one store when I was in town last night, and what's the point of having a TV if you're not going to watch it? Unfortunately all that's on is soap operas and talk shows, all boring, pointless stuff.

I stopped in at work to pick up some random crap for my room and that fucking kid was there again. Alexa was working and she told me that he stops in every day, and if I'm not working he asks for me. Supposedly they have asked him many times to leave, but he doesn't and we all know Alexa is too nice; she admits it herself; so she wouldn't be mean and make him afraid to come back. I just need to figure out where he lives, because then I can break in and teach him a lesson.

Have you ever sat in one spot for so long that your butt falls asleep? Well mine has, and it's all tingly and actually really annoying. This might be a sign I need to get up.

Hate, loathing, revulsion, detest, disgust . . . that is what I feel when I look at Emily. She talks so much shit and like 90% of it is lies, but of course there is always at least one person who believes every word she says. What's even worse is that the person she tells will exaggerate the story and tell five others and one will believe it and exaggerate more and tell five others and so on until I'm being told twenty different things from twenty different people, none of which makes sense.

I had a dream last night that I killed her, and the world thanked me for it. It was bloody and very brutal and the only other thing I remember is Isabella standing behind me cheering me on. I was a great dream. If only murder was that easy.

So, instead of killing her I'm going to go punch her. I've always wanted to just walk into a building punch someone and walk out; they do it in the movies all the time. Well, today I'm doing it. Pathetic her, she works in a grocery store in the deli, unfortunately I have to lean over the counter to do it, though I could always smash her head into one of the slicers, now wouldn't that be awesome?

I have to go pick up Isabella, she wouldn't miss this for the world.

July 17th

Long story short: I punched her, Isabella cheered, Emily cried, I laughed, and then we got kicked out. Emily chased us across the parking lot to the car and made sure I wasn't mad at her. Of course, I was and still am, but I told her I wasn't. She is so desperate for friends it makes her stupid, and I could say whatever I want and she'd eat it right up; literally.

On another note, I think I'm going blind. Well not totally but it gets harder and harder to see my computer screen each day, and sometimes I can't read labels on things. It sucks because I'm so not going to the doctor, so I've got to suck it up. That is one thing I used to hate doing, going to the eye doctor. They put those fucking eye drops in there and the whole world goes fuzzy, then for ten hours after you can't fucking see outside because the sun's too damn bright so you get a nasty ass headache and want to kill everyone. Or is that just how it goes for me?

How the hell did I get on the topic of eye doctors? Oh yeah, I'm going blind. I think I have a cure for it though; it's called alcohol, because when you are drunk the world is all blurry and then you don't know if it's the alcohol or your eyes, simple cure.

July 18th

So this week they have overloaded me with hours at work. I think I'm working like nine hours a day every day this week. It's crazy. I guess they just need the help, not like I'm complaining; I love the people I work with. They are so easy to joke around with; no one gets pissed off if someone takes the joke a little too far. We can usually mess around and not get much work done, but no one cares. I'm just excited that I get more hours with Alexa and Amber. Usually I get the night shift or middle shift, so we usually only pass or overlap for an hour. Today we got to work together for five hours and it was awesome. We hung a bra from for one aisle sign and threw gummies at the ceiling until they stuck. If someone asks, we don't know who did it, we didn't see anything.

Well it's late and I'm exhausted, so I'll get back to you first chance I get.

July 19th

Here's another blog moment for you:

Current mood: tired, happy, pissed, relieved, sore

Unfortunately in blogs you can't have more than one mood, and since this isn't a blog, I can have as many moods as I want.

Where to start.

Let's see.

Okay, so today at work I was attempting to put out all these boxes of supplies and stuff, and I was hidden behind the huge stack in a corner collapsing some of the empty boxes. Well, some damn kids thought it would be funny to knock the stack over, but they didn't realize I was behind it. Anyway, they pushed it over and lucky for me my one manager was right there and ran over to help me get out from under the boxes. Some of them fuckers were heavy. As a natural response I went to go beat the shit out of the little kids, but she wouldn't let me because I'd get fired for sure. Which is why I'm relieved that she saved me and my job. But I'm also pissed that the kids did it, and that I couldn't beat the crap out of them. I'm sore because of getting hit with all those boxes and I'm happy because they gave me tomorrow off. I'm pretty sure I sprained my wrist because it's so swollen right now and it's killing me. Better pop a Vicodin and go to bed; plus the keyboard isn't helping with the pain.

July 21st

Well my one day off didn't last very long because they called me in anyway. The new girl is so damn slow they needed someone else to cover her for back up on register and to fix all the mistakes she made when she was putting stuff out on the shelves. My wrist was and still is very swollen, so they had me stay on register all day because it's a light duty kind of task, the only bad part was that I had to work by her side all night. She is so weird; she talks as slow as she rings register. I'm pretty sure she thinks we are friends, she started wearing all black and telling me about various tattoos and piercings she wanted to get, all of which make me cringe just thinking about, she is not pretty in the least. After a while I couldn't take it anymore, since I didn't have to do anything she assumed she didn't either, which was a wrong assumption because there were two or three shopping carts full of stuff to be put out, and instead she stood there and talked to me. I was dumb enough to stand there for an hour and then I got so fed up I went outside for a cigarette, and I'll be damned, the fucking kid was out there! I'm surrounded by annoying morons!

I sat on the bench, he sat on the bench. I went into the store, he went into the store. He followed me like a damn puppy dog, except puppies are cute, he's not. Eventually I hid in the stock room and he left, then I had to go back on register with the slow poke.

And pretty much the same thing happened today, I got stuck on register, she talked about the same damn things, I left, then later he stopped by followed me, I hid, he left, then back to register. My life is one of those horrible dreams that keeps coming back.

Yesterday I got stuck on register again and it was the same thing as the last two days. The slow poke talked and I ignored her. I got work done and she didn't. Today I told them there was no way I was staying up there. I'd be backup, but I just wanted something else to do to get me away from her. I should have known though, that I would have to keep running up there to back her up every five minutes when her line got too long. The first two times I went up she talked to me and I decided to be polite and pretend to listen to her, but I'd heard it four days in a row, so after the first few times of pretending to listen, I just walked away while she was talking.

Not a single person who works there likes her, but the managers pity her for being retarded, so they won't fire her. I told them that she's a waste because she lets her line get so long and then she calls for backup and then two people end up dropping what they are doing to get rid of the lines. The customers get pretty pissy if they have to wait in line too long. I guess pity overpowers common sense. If I had my way she'd be long gone by now.

July 26th

You know, I feel like those girls in that movie who make a book of all the girls in their class and say bad shit about them. Except I don't have pictures of the people I talk shit on, and I don't talk shit on everyone, just most people.

I will be so happy when this week is up; I have almost sixty hours in eight days! I told them to hire more people, but everyone (except the weird chick) is like family and they don't want anyone to invade that. Fine then, give me the hours, make me have no life. It's been almost a week since my last drink, I'm dying here!

I feel like such an old person, I come home from work, take a nap, get up, take a shower, write and then go back to bed, I do nothing but sleep when I'm not working, it's pathetic. Speaking of sleep, it's "nuh nite time." Alexa has me hooked on saying that. Don't you dare repeat it, that's our thing, not yours!

I go nuh nite now!

Skipped work today. Actually, technically I slept in and missed the first four hours. I could have gone in late, but I didn't feel like it. They're not going to fire me . . . they like me too much. Even though I mess around a lot, and some days don't get very much done, when it comes down to really needing something done I am the fastest and most effective person at getting the job done. They won't get rid of me, I mean too much to them.

I'm considering taking the day off tomorrow too. It's the weekend and it's about time I get some semblance of my life back.

I heard Taylor was having a big bash of some sorts, and it just figures that she didn't invite me. I always find out about these things at the last moment and have to change my plans because who in their right mind is going to pass up on free beer?

And maybe, just maybe, I could make some money at this party. High school kids are always trying to find drugs and shit. I'll have to call my guy and order up some yummy's for the children!

July 28th

We are invisible children. Yes we are. Our parents do not see us, our teachers do not see us, our co-workers do not see us, the people who we think are our friends do not really see us. I mean they see us with their eyes but with nothing else. There is more to us than the eye can see, there is more below this tough exterior, there is a real person under here. It might be hard for you to understand or even imagine what I am talking about but if you ponder it long enough you might get it.

So I did go to work today for a little bit but then I faked sick and went home. When I was just about to get in my car this extremely old lady comes up to me and says "You better not walk alone. Don't you dare walk alone." I was and still am confused as all hell. It makes no sense. Was she senile or was it a real warning? I guess I will find out eventually.

July 29th

Dare not walk alone.
Dare not walk alone.
Dare not walk alone.
I still don't get it!

July 30th

The kid: I love you.

Me: Yeah okay, whatever.

The kid: I'm so in love with you it hurts.

Me: Look asshole, fuck off.

The kid: I love you. I love you so much.

Me: Leave me alone you fucking stalker.

The kid: I love you, doesn't that mean anything?

Me: You can say you love me over and over, but until you prove it, it means absolutely nothing, and since I won't ever give you the chance to prove it, you don't love me. Now go away.

And . . . He left.

What a pain in the ass.

Did I ever mention the kid's name is Nick? I'm pretty sure I did . . . but that was a while ago. I'm going to call him "the kid," but if I ever mention Nick, it's the same pain in the ass.

4 months left

I sat with Madison today while she killed herself. She called me earlier yesterday and asked if I would stay the night with her and be there when she did it. It was sad because she could have asked any of the other girls, but she asked me. I actually felt bad because I was never anything special to her. I never went out of my way to talk to her or be nice to her. Looking back, I regret not being a better friend to her.

We got up really early before her mom would wake and went into the bathroom. That house has the most beautiful bathroom I have ever seen. In the center is an enormous sunken bathtub with silver faucets and bench seats. At first I thought she was going to drown herself in it, but Ashlyn had already taken that idea, so I was clueless. Instead she made herself a cocktail of pills in her mom's medicine cabinet. Madison's dad had left them sometime last year for a younger, better version of her mom. And since then her mom has been on so many medications for depression and stuff to help her sleep. It was actually a really good idea for Maddie to die that way, a gentle passing for a gentle person.

She did fill the bathtub with water though; it was her insurance that nothing would go wrong. First she took a bunch of calming pills and then the sleeping pills followed. After the second handful she didn't look too good and I thought for sure she would throw up, but the sleeping pills were so strong they knocked her out. I'm not sure if she had a seizure or what, but she hit her head on the tub and sunk below the water. If the pills didn't kill her, the water would. It's always good to have a backup.

Soon as I knew she was out cold I got out of there. I didn't want her mom to see me there, and I didn't want to see her mom. I could only imagine what that lady would do when she found Maddie.

I've been feeling kind of down since this morning. I don't think its guilt; because that's not one of the emotions I'm capable of. It might be regret that she did it or maybe some other emotion I can't even describe. I think I need to just relax for the rest of the day, take it easy for a while.

3 months and 27 days left

I actually went to Maddie's funeral today. I hadn't planned on going to any of their funerals; I thought that Ashlyn was the only one who had earned my being there since she did go first. I guess I was still feeling down about watching her die.

I did notice that her mom wasn't there. Rumor has it that when she found Maddie's body she had another complete mental breakdown and the neighbors heard her screaming, so they came running. At first the cops arrested her because they thought she killed Maddie, but the autopsy showed differently. I guess because she was cleared of all charges and then admitted to some special mental facility.

Surprisingly though, Maddie's father was at the funeral. He was the last person I expected to see there. I hated him because, even though it was from a distance, I saw what his leaving did to Maddie and her mother. As I was leaving I walked behind him and leaned in and whispered, "It's all your fault." He turned around and looked at me, but I just walked away. I could hear him sob as I headed toward my car. Let him feel like shit for the rest of his miserable life, see if I care, he deserves it.

Emily called me to hang out after the funeral, but I just ignored her phone call. I don't know where she got the phone from or whose it was because I still hadn't turned hers back on, and I'm not planning on it, I just didn't want to talk to her.

August 5th

The college students started moving back into town today. We were so busy at work because they always forget stuff and they need groceries or kitchen supplies for their apartments and dorm rooms. I can't tell you how many hot guys I saw. Damn they are fine!

As usual "the kid" came in several times to bother me. He's always trying to ask me out or give me gifts, like flowers or jewelry are going to make me change my mind. The flowers go to whoever grabs them before they leave work and the jewelry gets sold down the street for a small percent of what he actually paid. But the extra cash is always nice to have.

Unfortunately, both Alexa and Amber have decided they think he's cute, so they don't warn me anymore, so much for their help.

Alexa is married and Amber's had the same boyfriend for the past three years, so neither of them are actually interested in being with him, just hooking the two of us up.

I don't want to be bothered by all that relationship crap; first dates, anniversaries, meeting the parents, having sex for the first time with that person, and so on. It's all awkward and easily avoided by simply staying single. There's also the matter of having to spend so much money all the time. If a girl lets the guy pay for everything all the time, eventually he will get pissed and that only leads to a nasty argument and someone getting hurt. It's so much simpler to be single and not have to deal with all that crap.

I don't know how a person can stay in one relationship for an entire life; the fights would have driven me crazy. I mean after about a month of being with the same person you really start to notice all their flaws and bad habits and you just want to strangle them. Imagine that building up over the years, having to go through everyday putting up with those annoying faults. I wouldn't be able to take it, maybe I'd put up with all the crap for a few months, but a year, ten years, thirty years, fuck that. I'm so glad I will never have to worry about it; I won't be around that much longer anyway.

August 6th

Are you pondering what I'm pondering? I seriously doubt it because that would mean you are in my head which is just really creepy.

And now you may be asking, "What are we going to do tonight brain?"

Well, my readers, we are going to take over the world.

Or rather we are going to this frat party I heard about at work today. A bunch of drunk, hot, college guys all in one house, it's every girls dream. Another good thing about tonight is the fact that college girls don't fight, they either don't know how or simply don't want to break their precious nails. They are such easy targets to pick on.

3 months and 23 days left

Remember back a week or two ago when that lady came up to me at my car and she said about the walking alone thing? Well I'm thinking it was a warning, though I have no clue how she could have known what was going to happen.

So when I was leaving that frat party a few guys followed me out. I had definitely made some enemies there so I figured they were just trying to scare me. I ignored them and kept walking, but when I got to my car they ran at me. I had no idea what they were going to do, but I had my guesses and none of them ended up good for me.

I'm assuming they didn't know what they were doing because the punches hurt, but not nearly as bad as I had expected. Let's just say that for big guys they punch like girls. The blood, bruises, and scrapes didn't hurt near as much as it hurt when they set in on my car. One of the guys grabbed a pretty large rock and threw it through my windshield, and of course, the tires got slashed too.

I'm not even mad that I got my ass kicked because I did kind of deserve it, but my car did nothing to them!

Now don't get me wrong here, I did like my car, but now I have an excuse to get a new one!

Everything can be repaired but why fix something when your dad is loaded?

Time for me to go shopping!

I called my dad yesterday, and told him I wrecked my old Honda. When I got up this morning there was a blank check sitting on the kitchen counter.

I spent most of the night online looking for a good car and I found a few I was interested in. I already set up a meeting for today with one guy to look at his car.

My plan is to write the check out to myself, cash it and whatever is left over after paying for the car is all mine. I figure I can get away with keeping at least a thousand dollars for myself, so a huge shopping spree will be coming up soon. I could be nice and buy my girls some new tattoos or piercings, but I'd rather be greedy and keep it all for me.

Alexa is here now to give me a ride. I hate being a burden to other people, but she offered, so I took her up on it.

August 11th

I wish you could see my new car . . . and hear it too! It's a 1999 Super Sport Camaro! This guy had four of them and wanted to get rid of one, so he would have space for a Firebird. Between the new exhaust, headers and everything else he put in that thing, it's a sweet-ass car. If you don't know what I meant by that, the car is louder and faster than if everything was stock and straight from the factory. It is one sexy beast, and if anyone touches it they will be losing those fingers.

August 12th

Emily heard somewhere through the grapevine about my new car and called me to say that I should come pick her up and give her a ride. That is definitely not going to happen. I'm not going to put the extra miles on the car or waste gas to go all the way out there for no reason other than to give her a ride. Fuck that. Plus I don't want her lard ass ruining my shiny leather seats, and she's always snacking on something. With my luck she'll dump her drink or drop crumbs everywhere. Hell no, that's not happening! Stay out and stay away from my baby!

August 13th

Today's topic is perverts at work. Coworkers to be specific.

When you first start at a job you usually don't know anybody so you kind of keep to yourself and just do what you have to until it's time to go home. Eventually you get to know the people better and you talk more and once you really start to feel comfortable you can joke around, which is great . . . until someone takes it too far.

I work with two dirty ass guys. One just so happens to be the head manager for our store. He is constantly suggesting we wear short skirts and low cut tops to work and then he stares at us all day. He's old, he's married, and he's probably harmless.

Now on the other hand, the second dirty guy is not so harmless. He's newly divorced and very horny. Every day is an invitation to come over to his apartment and get drunk and sleep over. Basically he wants to get girls drunk and rape them when they are sleeping. I'll pass on that offer. Plus the whole time he's at work he's telling us what he would love to do to us if he ever got us alone. I'm going to start carrying pepper spray from now on.

What a weird, weird, crazy strange day.

So I was at work, and I was the only person on register. It was a slow day, so I would ring someone up and then stand there for ten minutes or so until the next person came along. No one had come up for a while so I was playing a game on my phone and out of the corner of my eye I saw someone start to unload their cart onto my counter. I rung them up, subtotaled it and looked up to tell them their grand total. I'll be goddamned, it was my mom! I stuttered to tell her what she owed, she handed me the cash. I counted out her change and she left. It was so weird! She didn't even recognize me!

After that I needed a break, so I went inside the office to get my cigarettes and I hear this lady outside yelling at the head manager. My mom again.

"That inked up slut didn't give me all of my change! I want my money and I want her fired! How could you hire such a nasty whore like that anyway?"

I couldn't breathe. So that's what she thought of me?

The manager returned all of her change and came to talk to me.

"What happened? Why didn't you give her all her change?"

"I guess I was just nervous"

"Why in the world would you have been nervous?"

"That was my mom, and she didn't even realize I was her daughter."

He didn't know what to say and neither did I. There was nothing more to say. Lucky for me he sent me home early.

I got home and snuck in. I wanted to die. I wanted to destroy this horrible body I was in.

I feel better now. I'm calm.

Only a little over 3 months to go . . . . I can make it.

August 16th

3 months and 15 days left

So they didn't fire me . . . yet. They did, however, remove me from register duty and put me in the back stock room where no one will see much of me. Their reason behind taking me off register permanently is so that incase my mom comes back to the store to check and see if they got rid of me or not.

I wonder what she would say if she only knew I was her daughter. It just adds to my point that our parents don't know us. They don't know a single thing about us.

Ten hour shifts the next few days. My new position requires longer hours and harder work, so if I'm not back tomorrow I promise I will be soon.

August 19th

Every night I go to sleep, and I wish I wouldn't wake up. Then morning comes around and I do.

It just sucks because I don't have all that much time left and there's so many things I really want to do. My parents stopped putting money on the kitchen counter for me, probably because I just got that car, which means now I do have to work to be able to afford to go out and do things.

I pity those people who have to live paycheck to paycheck and are constantly paying bills. It sucks to be them, but lucky for me, I'll never know what it's like. At least not for long.

So I reread what I wrote the other day and I realized I sounded so weak. Don't you dare think I'm going soft, it's just that when you are so tired everything seems to come crashing down on you all at once.

I know that you know what I mean. You come home from work or school or whatever and everything feels like its going wrong. Maybe you will be pissed off and punch holes in walls, or maybe you will have a few drinks, or maybe even cry yourself to sleep. Everyone's done it . . . well except the crying part . . . I don't cry. And if I did I wouldn't tell you anyway. I wouldn't want you to think lesser of me than you already do.

I finally have a few days off of work, and I'm planning to catch up on all the drinks I missed out on when I was slaving away.

Isabella took the night off from her job, and I think she had mentioned about heading to the city. One of the guys she used to hook up with is a bartender in one of the clubs there so he can get us in and serve us. It's a great idea until they switch bartenders and the new one cards us. Then it's out on the street and possibly running from the cops. (Not that I haven't done that before.)

It's getting late . . . or should I say early? No matter which you prefer it's the perfect time to go to a club.

August 22nd

Well we didn't get kicked out last night, but I did end up running from the cops. The cops were just pissed because I threw and empty beer bottle on the hood of their cruiser. Again luck was on my side and I got away. I guess I'm just good like that.

Isabella went home with her bartender boy. The second we got in there he clung to her like a fat kid clings to his last candy bar. I guess he really likes her, but I know she's not interested. Basically she wants a friend with benefits and a few other bonuses to go along. If he wasn't a bartender I guarantee she wouldn't be sleeping with him, unless of course he worked at a shoe store . . . then she might marry him just to get all the free shoes she wants. That girl has an entire room filled with shoes!

Why am I talking about shoes? I don't even like them. They cost money and some hurt. I like pain, but I want to cause it myself.

Jamie just called and wants to meet and talk. I'm sure it's just nonsense talk, but I'm going anyway just so I can get out of here for a while.

August 28th

Bang
Beep Beep Beep
Bang
Beep Beep Beep
Bang
Beep Beep Beep

I love making car alarms go off!

You might be asking yourselves where the hell have I been the past week . . . well, it's a long story . . . maybe not that long . . . anyway here it is:

I met with Jamie at the shitty little dinner in town (the same one we went to after Ashlyn's funeral if you remember back that far). She basically wanted to say that she heard about some of the things the other girls and I were doing and she wanted to warn me that eventually I would get caught and get in big trouble. Blah blah blah. I heard it before. So when I left just to make a point, I pulled the baseball bat out of my car and started smashing it on random cars in the parking lot. I must have set off enough alarms because it was so noisy that I didn't hear sirens. The cops showed up and arrested me . . . fucking assholes.

In jail you get one phone call. It took me a while to decide who to call, and in the end I called Emily. She was my best friend and all . . . at least she's supposed to be. I know she has lots of money even though she claims she doesn't, and I figured she'd bail me out because that's what best friends do. Boy was I wrong.

I called that dumb whore and she goes "well this movie just came out in theaters and I really want to see it, so I can't lend you the money." And she fucking hangs up on me! Does it cost a million dollars to see a movie? NO! She's rich as shit and can't lend me a couple hundred bucks for bail? Oh that pissed me off!

So a couple days later I get another phone call. Isabella this time. She's the only person left that I can think of and who I know is reliable. She can't make it until the next morning but she promises she will be there and I will be out.

She kept her promise and I got out and now I'm here telling my story.

See it wasn't that long of a story, now was it?

August 30th

Court yesterday. All I got was a little fine and a spanking. Just kidding about the spanking.

I tried to pay Isabella back but she didn't want the money . . . she said she wouldn't need it where she was going. It's a very good point, one that I never would have thought of.

Driving home through town I saw "the kid" riding around on his skateboard in the parking lot in front of where I work. It's been a while since I've seen him, I bet he misses me. I sure as hell don't miss him.

I was definitely not looking forward to today. Isabella has grown on me, and I've come to like her a lot. For while I was considering going to her house and telling her not to do it, I wanted her to wait, someone else could go instead. I called her cell but she didn't pick up, so I called her house and her mom informed me that she and Stacey went to the dance studio in town to practice.

When I got to the studio Stacey was sitting outside crying. I'm not very good at consoling people, so I just sat next to her and waited until she was calm.

"She shot herself. Isabella shot herself. We were just upstairs dancing and the next thing I know she pulls out a gun and shoots herself. It happened like five minutes ago, the cops are on their way."

I was too late; I didn't make it on time.

So I sat with Stacey until the cops got there, and the ambulance came too. She had to tell them what happened at least four times and by the end she was a mess all over again. I ended up having to take her home and then come home myself.

Do you ever think to yourself, if this hadn't happened where would I be now? Or, if I had only been five minutes earlier, would that have changed anything? It sucks when you question yourself because you think that if you had corrected all the mistakes you made, if you had done this or not done that, where would you be, what would your life be like. Would it be better? Would it be worse? I don't know. It's all too complicated for me.

September 2nd

School started yesterday, but I obviously didn't go. It's only college, and it's so not important. Maybe I'll go today, I don't have class until two, but then again I'm not really in the mood.

I've been so tired lately and everything gets on my nerves. I hate bitching at people who have never done anything to me, but I just can't help it. What makes it worse is that sometimes I can't get away quick enough, so they end up suffering my rage. It really sucks for them because most of them have never seen me like that, and they don't know how to react. I actually made April cry last night because I was screaming at her, and I don't even remember why.

Emily just called me to ask why I wasn't in class yesterday. When we registered for classes she made sure that she had at least one class with me. I told her to fuck off and then I hung up. I'm sick of dealing with her shit. I hope she dies.

2 months and 27 days left

I should not have come to school today. "The kid" is in two of my classes. It just figures that he would sit next to me and try to talk. Then on top of that, he invites himself to lunch. Emily, Stacey and I were just sitting there and he comes over with two of his goonies and sits down. He introduced them as Justin and Kristopher. Justin is a loud, athletic looking guy; he's almost handsome but has the big brother look to him. Kristopher needs to get a hold of some acne medicine and a paper bag, he's really ugly, and he's a hopeless romantic. He was trying to seduce Stacey with poems and songs, but lucky for him, she just ignored him, if not I'd have to get rid of him and quick. I'm pretty sure Emily wants to bang him, she just looked longingly at him, but when she left to go to the bathroom he made a comment about "the whale." I couldn't help but laugh. You would too if you could only see her.

September 4th

I really do hate that kid. Today he asked me why I have all the scars on my arms. It made me so mad because it's none of his damn business. He kept asking and then for a while he stopped. Then he said, "You know they have help lines for that." The only thing I could think of to do was punch him, instead I shoved him backwards off his chair and left. He doesn't know me and he's never going to. That shit's just fucking rude.

September 5th

Again, I skipped my classes today. I wasn't in the mood to deal with "the kid's" shit. He's one of those people who says what he's thinking and doesn't care how what he says affects those of us around him. It's like when you see someone that has something in their teeth you will most likely not say anything and try to ignore it, which is almost impossible because your eyes are just drawn to it. He, on the other hand, will tell them immediately. So if you were sitting there the whole time trying to ignore it and he comes along and tells them, you end up feeling like the biggest jerk in the world. Then you have to try to convince them that you never even noticed it. I hate people like him. I hate him.

September 6th

Lunch table invasion again today. I can't take this damn guy anymore!

The first thing he says to me is, "I haven't seen you at the dollar store lately, where have you been?"

I didn't have to explain anything to him, but for some odd reason I did. "I work in the back now, so you won't see me anymore."

"Why'd they do that? Move you back there, I mean."

"A change of scenery I guess." He doesn't need to know the real reason they moved me.

"I miss seeing you. Do you want to hang out tonight?"

"Yeah okay . . . NOT! I can't stand you! Hell no."

Then the stupid little puppy boy followed me to my car and halfway home until I stepped on the gas and lost him.

September 7th

One of my professors today read some cheesy quote about how life is too short and yadda yadda yadda and you only live once and blah blah blah. I heard what he had to say, but I didn't really listen and process it until later at lunch.

I was off in my own world thinking while the rest of them were hanging out and talking. It hit me then that he was right! Life is too short, especially when you are working on a time line like me.

"I quit," I announce.

They all looked at me like I was a ghost. It was the first thing I said all day.

"I'm quitting my job today. Fuck it, I want to have fun."

I left the university and drove down to work. I walked in, emptied out my locker, walked to the front and said, "I quit. I'm out. See you around."

September 10th

The night I quit my job someone broke in there and stole several thousand dollars from the safe. Yes, I let the combination slip to a few people. Yes they all knew that there are no cameras or alarms, and no I didn't do it. But everyone thought I did.

I got home from school the next day and the cops were sitting outside waiting for me. I guess someone had told them to talk to me about the break in. They took me into custody and took my fingerprints to compare them to all the fingerprints on the safe's keyboard. I have never touched the safe so they couldn't find any prints of mine on there. And so they had to release me. Those bastards are going to suspect me for everything now!

What if I were to compare myself to the Mona Lisa? She's not drop dead gorgeous or nasty-ass ugly, and I could probably say the same for myself. But what really makes me want to compare us is that in the painting, she has the slightest smile on her face, it's just barely considered a smile. Now I'm thinking, is she happy, is she just posing or is she only pretending to be happy so everyone around her believes that little lie of a smile and doesn't bother her with pointless questions about what's wrong or what she is thinking. I wish I could keep that kind of face on, and I thought I could; until today.

We moved our lunch party to a different building so we could be alone, but he found me again today at lunch and of course sat down. It just figures that his idiots were there too. Justin; all silent and mysterious (it's just a front ladies; he's soft on the inside). And I swear Kristopher really likes Stacey, not that she has to worry about it, she only has to put up with him for a few more weeks.

Anyway, so I just ignored him and continued to pretend to listen to Emily bitch and complain about how fat she thought she was and how ugly she was and blah, blah, blah. Like I give a shit what she thinks.

Then she gets up and just leaves. He looks at me and says, "You can stop pretending to listen now." For the first time since he ever spoke to me I fixed my full attention on him. "I know you weren't really paying attention to her." Okay, I'll give him some credit; the boy's a little smart. "You get this look on your face when one of your friends is talking to you and you want to give them the impression you care when you really couldn't give two shits." Wow, major bonus points, you may have just passed this class.

And what if he figures out what's going on with all my friends dying? What if he figures it out and tries to stop us, tries to stop me? What if he stops me and I can't go through with it? I will have to let my girls down. Never, I won't let him. Simple solution is that I avoid him at all costs so he can't pick up anything else. "And there! That look!" What look? Uh oh what look? "That's the look you get when something is bothering you, but you don't want anyone to know something is wrong. It's like a mix between a blank stare and an attempt to smile." Shit, he's got me all figured out; doesn't he? "You know who you remind me of?" No, I obviously can't read minds like you. "The Mona Lisa. She's got that same face as you." Never thought I'd be compared to a famous painting, should I be flattered? There were a million things I could have said to him, a million rude things, but I kept them to myself. Now I know you're thinking, smack him or tell him go to hell and there I was not doing or saying anything. Something must be wrong with me, must be. I looked at him and it was weird, for the first time since he started bugging me, I really looked at him. The hair that I thought was a shaggy mess before, today seemed to be a halo in the sunlight on his head. His blue eyes were deep, so deep and calming. I didn't want to look away. So I did the only thing I could; I kissed him.

At first he seemed shocked, let me tell you that I was shocked too, then his hands wrapped themselves in my hair and held me there, the moment lasted an eternity and I almost wished it wouldn't end, but it did. When I opened my eyes Emily was standing behind Stacey and the two of them were open mouthed in shock, they had of course seen it all. Justin and Kristopher both cheered and clapped, and then I did another thing I never did before, I blushed. Then I grabbed my stuff and ran all the way to my car, driving as fast as I could, I got home in record time and locked myself in my room.

I'm sitting in my room, staring at my computer screen, still wondering what came over me. Do I like him? Is that even a possible emotion for me? Is this a possible love emotion or just lust? I'm betting on lust, I'm hoping its just lust. I guess it couldn't hurt to follow through with that kiss, what's a few more good fucks before I die? Right?

Well, Nick and I made our relationship official today at lunch. He came over and sat down again and had his stupid, big grin on. "You know you can't ignore me, especially since I know you like me."

I glared at him and said, "My, aren't we full of our self?"

Him and his stupid ass grin, I just want to punch him . . . or kiss him.

"I'm not full of myself, I know you like me and I know I like you, so what are you doing Friday night?"

"Locking myself in my room and avoiding you."

"Great! I'll be by around 8 to pick you up."

"Don't bother, I won't answer the door."

"Don't worry, I'll let myself in."

"I'll lock the door."

"I'll break it down."

"I'll call the cops."

"I'll let myself get arrested, but I'll come back as soon as I get out."

Fuck, I kissed him.

"So you're my girlfriend now?"

"Don't get too used to that word."

"Girlfriend. Girlfriend. Girlfriend," he chanted.

"I'll punch you."

He just laughed.

September 15th

I feel like I am in some fairy tale romance movie. He's got the look that every girl wishes her man would have, clean cut but a little rough around the edges. He says all the right things at all the right times, and that "bros before hoes" saying, well it's totally opposite for him. If I was the marrying type, he would be the one.

I think I love him . . . at least a little.

2 months and 14 days left

Love.

Now you are probably thinking I'm extra crazy because we have only been together for three days, but it's true. We have spent every second together since that first day, and I couldn't be happier. I thought maybe I would feel smothered, but so far I've just felt happier than I ever have before. I feel complete.

I am going to love him until the day I die.

Someone pray for me to have the strength to go through with this. I can't stop, for now we are so close to the end.

September 20th

Stacey and Emily are concerned. They say I'm changing. They say they have never seen me this way before, so happy, so alive.

All I can tell them is don't worry about it. The looks on their faces show that they don't like what I said, and they don't trust me anymore.

What do I do to get them to trust me again? I will not let them down, but I also don't want to lose Nick. It's a double edged sword and I'm standing on the tip waiting to see which way I will fall.

September 22nd

They are still very worried about me. Stacey sat me down and tried to explain the meaning of love to me.

She said, "Love is not just a feeling . . . it's also an ability. To love someone you have to start by loving yourself. You have to be able to give every part of yourself to that person and trust them that they won't hurt you. Love is not being able to say no to that person. Love is giving up in a fight to make the other person happy. Love is never getting your way and not always being happy because what makes the other person happy makes you miserable. Love is knowing deep down inside that the two of you were created for each other. It's the thought of being with that person tomorrow that gives you the strength to go on today. It's always remembering every moment together but not letting a bad memory ruin a good day. That's not even half of the things I could say about love, but I'll stop there. I think you get my point."

She left and I just sat there thinking. I didn't know what to say. I know inside my heart that I love him, and that's all there is to it.

September 23rd

Every minute I spend with him I realize more and more that we were meant to be together. As cheesy as it might sound, it's like we know what each other is thinking. He finishes my sentences and it's like he can read my mind. I can be thinking something and all he has to do is look at me, and he says exactly what I was thinking out loud.

You've got to be thinking that it's all too soon, it can't be for real, but it's not too soon and it is for real.

Tonight is our first night apart since we've been a couple. He's a big family-oriented person and like once a month they all get together and go out for dinner. I politely declined, there is no way I am ever going to meet his parents. That's just too fucking weird for me. He claimed that it was very important to him, so I told him to just go without me. I said I had some things to do, and that I wouldn't be bored, so he left, and here I sit.

I lied. I am bored. Actually I'm paranoid as all hell. I keep thinking what if the waitress is hot, and he gets her number so they can hang out sometime? What if he runs into an old fling and forgets all about me? I have no right or reason to be thinking that. He always tells me that I'm the only girl for him. I guess my overreaction is just a girl thing.

I wonder how married women do it. I bet everyday they battle their own minds wondering what their husband is doing. I'd go crazy for sure. And there's no easy way to ask him everything he did that day without being suspicious.

It's just like that living pay check to pay check thing, I'm glad I don't have to do it for long.

God I hope he gets back soon.

Last night we were hanging out and he was being so perfect. He took me out to dinner and a movie; he bought me flowers and an expensive looking necklace. It was everything every girl could ever dream of.

We were back at my house, lying together cuddling, and I looked up at him and I had to say it, it just felt right. "I love you."

He didn't hesitate or pause, right away he says, "Love you too."

I was so relieved and happy that he didn't make the situation awkward. That of course lead to our first time doing you know what. It's always so weird the first time a couple has sex. I was worried what he looked like down there, and I was worried what he thought of me, but I guess he liked it. My only complaint is that he only pleasured himself. I didn't really get anything out of it, but as long as he was happy, then I was happy.

He stayed the night and left early this morning to run some errands. I didn't sleep much because I was doing a lot of thinking, and I've spent most of the day thinking about it too.

I said, "I love you," but he said, "Love you." Maybe to you that's not a big deal, but to me those are two totally different sayings.

When you say, "I love you" it means that you would do anything for that person; you would give up everything for them, maybe even die for them. They are your everything, your whole world.

On the other hand, "Love you" is what you say to close friends and relatives. You say that because you feel an obligation to say it, but you don't really mean it.

It's been bugging me since he said it, he probably only said it because he wanted to make me happy and that way he also knew it would better his chances at getting laid.

Maybe he isn't so perfect, maybe he's just a jerk. Maybe.

2 months and 2 days left

Nothing has changed between us, no weird awkward moments, he hasn't said the "L-word" again and neither have I. I'm pretty sure if he said it to me the way he did the other night, I would have cried. It just means that he's in this relationship for himself. It's a one sided relationship where only one person gets what they want and only one person is ever happy.

Ugh! Can I ever be truly happy? I already know the answer to that question, but just humor me.

There's nothing here for me anymore, so I'll just finish out my days and then I can rest in peace. No boys, no jobs, no school, no family, no worries. Stacey and Emily will be very happy to hear this.

October 1st

Anytime that we go someplace Nick usually drives. Today I took him on a cruise in my car. I'm pretty sure he was scared shitless because he didn't say a single word. We were flying through some back roads and when I came around this one turn I had to slam on the breaks. In front of me were cops and ambulances and fire trucks. Beyond them I could see that a vehicle had driven through the guard rail and down a good thirty foot drop. I couldn't see the car but I was betting it was on fire because black smoke was filling up the sky. There was no way I could turn around because there were cars lined up in both lanes as far back as I could see. I figured we'd be sitting there for a while so I shut off the engine and reclined in my seat.

Nick started talking about random shit and I was only half listening, I was busy staring at the broken guard rail. There were streaks of lime green paint where the car had hit and went down the bank. There was only one person I knew who had that color car.

In the middle of his one sided conversation I get out of my car and walk towards the broken guard rail. A cop stops me and says that I have to back up because at any moment the car could explode. I hardly heard a word he said.

I ask the cop, "Who is that? Who was in the accident?"

"We don't know, it's going to be hard to tell. There's not a lot left."

"Is the car a Jetta? A lime green Jetta?"

"Yeah, why do you know who it is?"

"Her name is Stacey. Stacey Kline."

I had to walk away. I couldn't stand there anymore. There was no where I could go but back to my car. Nick had the look he was going to say something, but I shook my head and he stayed quiet. I had to sit there in my car and watch the smoke go higher and higher. I kept praying to myself that she hadn't suffered.

I didn't even get to say goodbye.

October 2nd

A long, long time ago I was researching suicide online and I came across some website were someone had written, "A suicide kills two people." I didn't get it, I didn't understand; but now I do.

Stacey killed herself, but I feel like she took a part of me with her. There are so many things I wish we could have done together or things that I would have said to show her how much I appreciated her friendship.

Today I feel like I'm in a trance, like I'm on the outside looking in. We sat there yesterday for over three hours while all the authorities stood around and watched the car burn. I hated them; they could have at least tried to help her. I know that it was too late and I know it's what she wanted, but I didn't think I'd have to suffer it with her.

October 3rd

Stacey was on the news today. There were different parents arguing about how the township should put up caution signs so no one else has an accident there. I wanted to call them up and scream at them that it wasn't an accident, but why waste my breath?

It's done. It's over. And there's nothing anyone can do about it.

Funeral's tomorrow. I wonder if they even found anything left of her to bury.

October 4th

One tiny, tiny, little box, that's all they could scrape up of her. I bet the ashes aren't even her's. They are probably just random ashes from the car's interior.

I saw that on TV once. Theses sick people would give a family some random ashes and then used their dead loved ones body for experiments or black market organs. Those people deserve to die.

Emily is so goddamn clingy right now. I hardly get any alone time with Nick anymore. I didn't really notice she wasn't around that much, but now that Stacey's gone, she has nowhere else to go, no friends. This is the end of my peace and quiet or at least for twenty four days, then its peace and quiet all over again.

With her it's always the same conversations, boys and being fat. You think she'd come up with some new material, but I guess not.

October 8th

So ever since that day he didn't tell me he loved me we haven't had sex.

At first I thought maybe it was something I did, then I thought maybe it was something he did, then I thought maybe he didn't want to be forced to say the "L-word" again.

It's all too much thinking, but now I do know why. It's all because I went back to acting how I did before I was with him. It's a combination of him not saying "I love you" and Stacey's suicide. I know I have to go through with this, and now I know that there is nothing holding me back.

October 12th

I could kill her!

Fucking Emily was hanging all over Nick last night! She is the biggest slut I know! Why do I have to suffer just because she's too fucking ugly to find her own guys?

October 13th

Happy one month today for me and Nick. He brought me two-dozen roses to school today. I love roses, but pretended to hate them. Then we went to my car to drop off books and I practically jumped him. My lips just seemed to refuse to leave his. We ended up crawling into my back seat; luckily I was parked in the furthest spot from anyone else. I don't know what parts of us they would have seen, but it wouldn't have been pretty. And that's the end of what I'm going to tell you, I don't kiss and tell.

October 14th

School. School. School. I don't know why I even bother going anymore. Maybe it's for the fact that I would never get a break from Emily if I stayed home. We might have our classes together, but at least she can't talk to me. Dumb fat whore. I'm still pissed about her slutting herself all over my boyfriend.

I'm counting down my days and I've realized that the end is coming near.

My game plan from here on out is to spend as much money as possible. I'm going to spend every cent in my checking and savings account. I'm going to max out all of my credit cards. And if I still have some time left over after I do all that then I'll take whatever I find of my parents' money and spend that too.

My first thoughts of where to spend it are either on another piercing or another tattoo. Actually possibly I'll do both and that way I don't have to pick one.

I really want to get my tongue pierced, but I've always been scared of it. It's just weird thinking about some dude grabbing your tongue and jamming a giant needle through it. I won't be able to talk right for a week, but I'm doing it.

October 17th

I got the tongue piercing and I got a tattoo last night when I was out. Emily was begging me the whole time to borrow some money so she could get something too. I knew I wouldn't get paid back so I said no. It sounds kind of childish because my goal is to spend as much money as possible but I hate her so much that I don't want to waste any of it on her.

I also made an appointment for a week from tomorrow to get another tattoo. I am getting a huge pin up girl on my leg. I've always wanted one, so why not get one? I'm more that jealous of how pretty those girls look, so if I get one in a tattoo I can look at it every day!

So far I've had a pretty good start on spending all my money, tonight I'll go to the mall and see how much junk I can find to bring home.

1 month and 12 days left

Nick is beyond confused now. He says he feels like he doesn't know me anymore. Like I've changed so much I'm a totally different person. I don't really know what he's talking about. Maybe it's because Emily is always around now and so I have almost completely stopped talking. It's not worth even trying to get a word in because she never stops.

He texted me while I was in class this morning and all it said was, "we need to talk." Well, if that doesn't make your heart damn near stop. I'm pretty sure I had a panic attack because I couldn't breathe and I started shaking. I had to get up and walk out. There was no way I could sit there for another half hour and still leave that class sane.

When someone says that to you, you always expect the worst. I couldn't think of any reason he would be mad at me. I got to our lunch table and Nick and Emily were sitting there already. Emily was talking nonstop and Nick was looking around probably hoping I'd left class early. When he spotted me he got up and left Emily sitting there looking hurt that he had walked away from her. He grabbed me and we walked back outside to one of the benches where we could talk in private.

Basically, he told me that he understood why I would keep more to myself since Stacey died because he knew she was my best friend. He also said he sees why I have changed because Emily is always hanging around and it's hard to be myself when you have dead weight hanging on your arm at every second of the day.

He said he understood, but he didn't. He didn't realize that I was trying to pull myself away from him very slowly so he wouldn't be as hurt when my time came. He didn't understand a thing. But he promised he would get rid of Emily for a few days so we could have time just to ourselves. I was not going to complain about alone time with him.

With that he went to his next class, and I skipped out on the rest of the day to come home and write. Sometimes I feel like you, whoever you are, are the only person who really knows me and knows how I feel.

October 20th

Nick asked me to go on their family's annual Christmas vacation today. I almost got excited, but then I realized I wouldn't be around for this Christmas. So I nonchalantly looked at him and said, "Yeah sure." He took it the way I had hoped, like I was really excited but acting cool so Emily wouldn't say anything. She gave me a weird look as to say "you won't be here" but I just glared at her to keep her mouth shut. Then he went off all excited, telling me everything they do while they are away on vacation, it was hard not to be sad about not getting to go, but I tried, and you've got to give me some credit.

October 22nd

Yesterday was the start of several days free of Emily. Just me and Nick time. Unfortunately, all he has talked about since we got alone was this vacation for Christmas. The more he talks about it the more I wish I could go and the more I feel guilty for leading him on to believe that I'll be there with him, when really I won't. It's hard because how do you tell someone; sorry I can't go because I'll be dead by then. Well, honestly you don't. If I said that to him he wouldn't understand or he would think it was just a joke. So he can keep thinking I'll be there with him and hopefully I never have to see his face when he realizes I'm not the girl he thinks I am.

October 24th

Maybe this whole alone time with Nick wasn't such a good idea. When we first started going out it was fine because I was just getting to really know him, but now I feel like I do know him and instead of trying to learn more new things about him, I'm focusing on all his little things that he does which drive me crazy. Like every time he starts a sentence he has to clear his throat, or he's always twisting his hair around his finger when he's thinking. It's just those little things that have started to drive me crazy. I hate that in the beginning of a relationship everyone fakes who they are just so the other person will like them, but as they get to know each other more and as they become more comfortable around each other all the little ticks come out.

I think I need a break from him already. I need a break from everyone. I need a break from the world.

October 25th

Last day alone with Nick for a little bit.

I told him today that my friend Taylor was moving and that she asked me to come help pack up some of her stuff.

Really the truth is that I need to get away and she offered to let me come visit her for a few days and she'd get me so drunk I'd forget all about him.

Of course, being the understanding boyfriend he is, he didn't ask any questions. He just told me to have fun and be safe driving there . . . and right as he got in his car to head home he said, "I love you." Then he shut his door and drove away.

Now my head is going into a million different directions. I can't even think straight enough to write it all down for you. What? . . . When? . . . . Why? . . . . I don't know where to start.

I am going to Taylor's and hopefully she can distract me enough so I can clear my head and think like me again.

I'm back! Did you miss me? I bet you didn't!

Three days away with Taylor helped me clear my head a little, but not much. All I can think about is Nick. He really does love me, and now I feel so bad because I'm going to have to break his heart!

I did love him for a little while, but now I'm not so sure. At first I think I loved him because he was the only person who doesn't know what's really going on between me and my friends, so he's the only person who doesn't judge me and who sees me as a normal person. Now I don't think I did love him just because it's like Stacey said, it was too soon to tell and I was rushing for things to be perfect between the two of us.

I have a feeling things are going to be a little awkward between us now because I'll be the one not to say, "I love you." Why now? Why all of a sudden he loves me? It's been who knows how many days since I said it and now out of nowhere he says it. I don't know what to do.

Do I break up with him now so he doesn't get hurt later? Do I stay with him until the end? What do I do?

October 30th

I think I am more worried about getting hurt than hurting him.

I've decided that I am going to stay with him until the end. I don't want to see the look of betrayal and hurt and hate on his face if I break up with him. Plus, who wants to spend the last days of their life crying over some guy that never really meant anything to begin with? I don't.

All I have to do is act naturally and he will never see it coming.

Emily and I are going shopping today. She wants to get a new outfit to wear for her big day tomorrow. I'm almost sad it's her time, because then I will be by myself and who will bug me and who will I have to ignore? I guess I can't have my cake and eat it too.

At least I will still have Nick. After Stacey died, Kristopher stopped hanging out with us and soon after that Justin didn't show up anymore either. So it's just me and Nick, and Emily sometimes too; though she wasn't a very good third wheel. She tended to get upset when she thought we were ignoring her, which we did a lot.

I had hoped to scare the shit out of some trick-or-treaters tonight since it is my favorite holiday, but that kind of stuff is no fun to do alone and since Emily is being moody and only wants to think about herself, I can't have my fun.

The mall isn't all that bad though. At least on a day like today when all the little kiddies are out dragging their parents all over the neighborhood to get free candy which will make them hyper and make their parents regret taking them, the mall will be empty.

First she will drag me to Hot Topic, then Spencer's, and then the seasonal costume store. We never go into any other stores; they aren't good enough for me to wear their clothes, so I refuse to go in them. With my luck she won't find anything to wear and we will have to go to a totally different mall nearly an hour away just to satisfy her.

I wonder what is going to happen with all her stuff when she's dead. I never thought about it with any of the girls before, but it is a good question. I know that for myself, I'm planning to destroy and get rid of most of it, that way I won't be a burden to anyone. The only things that will be left in my room will be my bare mattress, with a suicide note laying in the middle and my computer, turned on and opened to this journal. It's a big chance I'm taking, because who knows if anyone will read this and who knows if they will obey my wishes. So if you are reading this off my computer then print it out and send it to an editor. Publish it for me. Another wish is that I am not buried with my girls; I don't think they deserve to be having their bodies in the same place as mine. Cruel but true, get over it.

November 1st

1 month left

I am celebrating today. This day should be a national holiday. I bet you forgot already just exactly what today is. It's the day Emily dies!

I told Amber that we have to have a party, she doesn't know why, but it's been a long time since the last party at her house, so it's time for another.

I don't know why this makes me so happy. Wait, no, I do, I lied. This makes me so happy because I am finally rid of her. You might or might not understand; I don't feel like explaining it to you. Just be glad that you will never have to run into her on the street, it would be an experience I would never wish on you.

November 2nd

We celebrated all last night. No one but me really knew why we were partying like we had never partied before, but I didn't care, it was the best night of my life.

I took Nick along because he had never met my other friends before. It seemed like he had a good time, but who knows? I'm no good at reading guys, so I can never tell what they are really thinking.

He asked me why Emily wasn't there and simply I said, "Who cares? The world is better off without her." Maybe that was saying too much or giving something away, but I was drunk so it sounded good at the time.

November 3rd

Nick: "Emily's dead!"

Me: "Oh really?"

Nick: "You don't even care? She didn't tell you anything?"

Me: "She tells me lots of things but I never listen . . . you know that. Where'd you hear this? What happened to her?"

Nick: "It was all over the news this morning. It looks like she made herself a cocktail of chemicals from her house. They said it ate her from the inside out and when they found her it wasn't a pretty sight."

Me: "Sweet."

Nick: "That's all you have to say is sweet?"

Me: "What else is there to say? I hate that whore. I'm glad she did it."

November 4th

0 months and 26 days left

Nick probably thinks I'm some psychotic bitch now because I'm happy my "best friend" killed herself. Whatever, he can think what he wants. I'm happy she's gone and I refuse to go to her funeral, she's not worth the gas it takes to drive there. I just think of all the times I did have to drive her ass around because she didn't have a license. I'm betting that my miles per gallon went down every time she got in my car because she added so much more weight to it. She is probably in hell right now fucking every dude she sees and lucky her, she doesn't have to worry about STD's or getting pregnant anymore!

It feels so good to be able to talk shit on her and not have it come back and bite me in the ass somehow. There is no chance for her to stumble across this while she's playing solitaire on my computer while I take a shower or go outside for a cigarette. There is no one for me to talk shit on her to that will go back and tell her everything I said. No more worries! No more drama! No more Emily!

November 6th

These long dreary days of my life are slowly coming to an end. I've spent all my cash and I'm working on the credit cards. I've ordered a ton of junk from the internet which won't arrive until after I'm gone. Knives, a gun, some rope, some pain killers, just a few things to remind everyone how we all died.

I hope when this is all said and done and my little journal here gets out to the public, people will understand why we did this. Our lives suck and no one made any move to help make it better.

It's everyone in the world's fault we had to do this. Is it so hard for parents to love their children and accept them for who they are? Is it so hard for a friend to lend an ear or a shoulder to lean on when they are needed? Is it so hard for a stranger to smile as you pass on a street? Is it really that hard to think of someone other than your lousy self for once? NO! It's not hard but none of those things ever happen! It's all your fault we had to do this! It's all your fault.

Now I'll bet a hundred bucks that starting tomorrow maybe you will be walking to work, or to class, or maybe you're in the mall and you pass a stranger who makes eye contact with you, and I bet you will smile back. Because in your mind you will be wondering if they feel the same way I do. Because a day, a week, a year from that day you passed them, maybe they will kill themselves and blame you all because you didn't fucking smile at them!

November 11th

I guess I was a little harsh the other day. But I'm not going to apologize. I've earned the right to be bitter.

I've been feeling a little guilty lately because I feel it's just not right for me to leave Nick without an explanation. I'll probably see him the day right before I do this thing and what's he going to think when the next day I turn up dead? I want so bad to tell him, but I can't. I know he will do everything in his power to stop me and I can't let that happen. I think what I have to do is write him a letter explaining everything and I'll put it in the mail either the day I do it or the day before, that way he will get it a few days later and he will know everything and not blame himself. I couldn't live with myself if he blamed himself for what I did, then again, I won't be living.

November 13th

0 months and 17 days left

Happy two months for me and Nick! How is it that girls remember all the important dates and the guys always seem to forget. He was acting like today was just any other day, but it really wasn't. It's the last anniversary we will ever share together, he doesn't know that and he doesn't need to either; yet. It is extremely frustrating though, you would think he is fully capable of remembering one day out of every month but I guess it's not possible for him.

He didn't even notice anything was wrong until he tried to kiss me and I didn't kiss him back. He asked me what was wrong and I replied with, "Nothing." Every time a girl says that there really is something wrong and either they don't want him to know or they want him to figure it out himself. He figured it out right away and spent ten long minutes apologizing before he took me out for a huge expensive dinner. It was nice, but not what I would have liked. I'd have been happier just being alone with him than going to a packed restaurant and having to sit for over an hour until we got our food.

Again, I know I can't always have my way, but getting it once in a while would be very nice.

November 15th

All Nick can talk about right now is this damn family vacation! It's getting harder and harder for me to pretend to be excited. He was telling me the entire game plan for the whole trip, a lot of the stuff sounded fun, but I probably would get frustrated having every single moment of the day planned out to the minute. That's no vacation, that's more like a school field trip.

I did luck out a little bit because I was getting worried that they would want to leave before it's my big day, but as luck has it, they leave ON my big day. All I have to do is pull it off before he comes to pick me up, and I won't have anything else to worry about.

He keeps bugging me and rushing me to pack my things because his parents want to make sure they have enough room in their car to get us and our belongings to the airport. A little weird, aren't they? I plan to pack a ton of clothing whether or not I would wear it on a trip or not, it's just helps me get rid of my belongings, it's less I will have to burn later and I'm sure his parents would be more than willing to give my clothes away to the needy. They seem like those types of people to me.

Fuck that. Let those goddamn lazy bastards fend for themselves; don't give to the needy or the poor! Make them get their own fucking jobs!

November 16th

0 months and 14 days left

I get my tattoo tomorrow!!!!

I hope you didn't forget, tomorrow is my day for my pin up girl tattoo. I am more than excited to get it done! I'll only have a couple weeks to look at it, but it's so worth it!

Nick's going with, maybe I can convince him to get one too! Wish me luck!

November 18th

Got my tattoo yesterday! It hurt so bad, and it took so long to do that when the guy was done Nick had to carry me to the car because my legs were asleep. He wasn't brave enough to get one for himself so he sat there and watched me. I think he was kind of disgusted by it, but I am always fascinated by it.

It snowed today, but only for a little bit. I really wanted to get one last snow ball fight in before it's my time, but I don't think it's going to happen.

There are a few things I have to do before I go, and so I'll be hinting to Nick to take me to do them. First thing on my list is paintballing. Hopefully, he takes me tomorrow.

November 19th

"What is that document you are always writing on your computer?" Nick asked as he tried to read over my shoulder.

"Oh nothing, I guess you can call it a diary, but I'd almost like to get it published and have others read it."

"Can I read it?"

"No."

"Why not?"

"Because I said so."

"That's not an answer."

"It's my answer and it's final."

I guess my tone said it all, so he just said, "Oh okay." He sat there quietly for a bit and then mumbled, "I will read it someday."

"No you won't"

"Oh, yes I will."

I don't think so.

November 20th

Nick's being very weird today. Last night we went out and played paintball for hours in the dark. He showered when we got back, but I waited until this morning. I had to take an extra-long shower because the paint was so dry it wouldn't wash off.

When I got out, he was sitting on my bed staring out the window, and he was definitely deep in thought. I barely touched him and he jumped.

"I gotta go," was all he said.

I didn't get a kiss goodbye or anything, it almost seemed like he didn't want to touch or look at me. Whatever, boys are weird.

"I love you," I muttered to the empty room.

"I know what you are doing. I know what's going on," he said.

"I don't know what you mean," I replied.

"Yes you do. All your friends killed themselves and it was your idea. You killed them. Do you know how sick that is? You disgust me."

"I didn't do it. It was . . . It was their idea," I practically sobbed.

"No it wasn't, and you damn well know it wasn't. You were behind it all," he shouted. "You are sick, you make me sick."

I didn't have a response to that, I just cried.

"What makes it worse is that they weren't really your friends. They just wanted to be like you, to fit in somewhere, and even worse than that, they had belonged somewhere, with other groups of people, other cliques and you forced them away from what they knew and loved. You were like a dictator, they practically worshiped you and you knew it. They would have and did do everything you wanted and told them to do."

"Ppppplease," was all I could stutter between the tears.

"You disgust me Kristen. You have no family. You have no friends. You're nothing to me or anyone else. I don't even know why I bothered to pursue you; it was a waste of my time. Why do you even bother to live anymore? You might not be better off dead, but the rest of us would be better off if you were, so do it, go die and I'll finally be free of you and you will be free of this world you hate so much. You'd be free of parents who would care and be there if you let them. Free of a great house and a great school providing you with even greater opportunities! Do it! Be free of it all!"

I wish I could be invisible.

"I hate you. I have never hated anyone more that I hate you right now. You deserve to die."

First I cried, but hearing this made me pissed, he said he loved me! "You think my life is perfect? Do you?"

"Here we go with that typical question. Yes, I think you would have the perfect life, if you let it happen, but you didn't. You fucked that up real good."

"How about you try being me for a day? How about you try living inside a storm, my storm — a black, spinning hurricane of hate, fear and self-loathing, then tell me my life's perfect. Try having your emotions go up and down and you have to go through it all, every waking moment. See how great of an outlook you have then."

"Stop lying. Stop lying to me. Stop lying to the world. Stop lying to yourself. You are ridiculous, do us all a favor and either lock yourself up or end it all now. I leave in a few days for my vacation, without you. And when I get back all my stuff better be returned to my home."

And he left, and I cried myself to sleep.

November 22nd

It's not like I lost something, because there was never anything for me to lose, but that doesn't stop me from feeling so alone.

We never would have married or had kids. It never would have gone further than the two months we were together. That doesn't stop it from hurting.

I loved him.

I still do.

November 23rd

0 months and 7 days left

I visited their graves today.

Was there truth in what he said? Were they really my friends?

I have never felt so alone. I feel like I have finally become truly invisible.

November 24th

0 months and 6 days left

Counting down the days until I can end my misery. I wouldn't want to let them down. If I really did murder them, then I do deserve to join them.

I've cried for four days now. I didn't know anyone could cry this much. Will these tears ever end?

November 25th

Why am I still crying over a stupid boy? Love is just not worth it. Girls, never fall in love, never let it happen okay? Promise me.

November 26th

0 months and 4 days left

I'm in a better mood today. Do you think maybe its better this way? See he broke my heart and I only have to suffer for a few days, but if I had broken his, he would have to live with that pain for years. Here I am caring about his feeling; never could I have imagined myself like this.

School let out today, we have off until mid-January. Not that I care, I only get the first few days and then I get the rest of my life off. Cool huh?

November 27th

Mom was making a turkey for Thanksgiving this morning. I have nothing to be thankful for, so I turned up the heat on the oven, the turkey caught on fire and came out all black and charred. The smoke alarms all went off, and I could smell that horrible smell of burnt bird all the way up in my room. Mandy came up to tell me they were going out to eat instead and asked if I wanted to come along. I didn't even bother to open the door, I just told her to go away. I was probably a little ruder than I should have been, but she went away. So what? Maybe I am a miserable fuck; you can just piss off.

December 1st

Today is the big day. Today is my day. My turn. This is what I have waited 8 long months for. I can't turn around now. It's down to me to finish this. I started it; I will end it. God, it's hard to believe that we've come so far. First Ashlyn, then Alicia. I guess I do miss them a little. Brooke, Madison, and Isabella who I could never forget. And Stacey and Emily who affected me more than they could ever know.

I wrote a note for my parents, just something to tell them how I feel. I was going to leave it in my room, but for some reason I feel like I need to keep it with me. They won't find it until they find my body. I don't really feel like sharing it with you, maybe someday someone will find this journal and publish it and as a closing statement or afterward; paste a copy of it in the end.

I guess this is the end of the road for us. It's been nice chatting to you. In a few hours I will leave my house and go down to the park. It was the place where my parents used to take us for walks when we were little. It's actually the place where I was nearly born, so I just thought it would be . . . creative to end it where it almost started. End my miserable life where it began.

Anyway, I have to get ready, have to get dressed. It's kind of funny, I'm dying tonight and I'm more concerned about what I'm going to wear and how my hair will look. Maybe I shouldn't have made fun of Emily when she complained about needing a new outfit for her day.

How do I end this? Do I just say goodbye? I guess that's all I can do. Goodbye and thank you for being the one who listened to me.

December 2nd

1 day overdue

FALIURE! I AM THE BIGGEST FAILURE EVER! I couldn't do it! I sat there for hours with that piece of glass in my hand and didn't move a muscle! I can't believe it! I thought of all the people to do it, I would be the best. Have it the easiest because I saw them do it, so it should have been easy for me to follow. Ridiculous! I can't believe myself!

Well I have slept all day and now it's time to try again. I refuse to give up. I got a good 14 hours of sleep, like the dead need rest. I almost smiled! Tonight I'm trying a different place. Our old house. The people just moved and it's back up for sale. I don't know how many people will want to buy it now, after a dead girl is found inside, but that's not my problem.

Cross your fingers for me. I will see you in the next life.

December 3rd

Third times a charm . . . I hope. I don't understand why I can't do this. It's not that hard to do. Just shove a sharp piece of glass into easily broken skin and watch the blood flow. Simple see? Now if only I could do it. I can't honestly tell you, or myself, why I can't do this, so I'm coming up with my own explanations. I think it's just that I haven't picked the right place to do it. The first two places just didn't have the right feeling. There was nothing there for me to love or hate. But tonight I have to perfect place and it's guaranteed to work. It has to. Want to know where it is?

It's Nick's house! The family left for vacation on the 1st so no one will find me until they get home. I love and hate that house just like I love and hate him! There is so much emotion there it's guaranteed to work!

I'm telling you the truth now; this really is the end.

December 7th

The cool, smooth surface of the glass between my fingers made me think twice. I can't do this! It was my third try and I still couldn't put myself through it, one cut and that's all it takes. How can someone be so miserable and yet so afraid to put one tiny piece of glass into their vein? It was pathetic; I was pathetic. Last week it was the thought of crashing my car, the week before was a hanging, but why couldn't I do it? And yet again, for one reason or another I sit here with opportunity in my fingertips and can't even move myself enough to put it into my flesh.

My keys jingled and clicked as I moved to lie down on the pavement. The cold, rough slab of concrete rubbed against my skin, and I shivered as the wind blew around me. This was way too easy. To just lay here and wait for it to come, wait to die. Giving up is so easy compared to forcing the inevitable. It was so cold just lying there on the sidewalk. No one passed for hours as far as I knew. Anyone hardly ever came here in the winter; no one will ever know I'm gone until they get back.

Taking a deep breath I let the cold glass slide into my skin. The pain was sharp at first, and then it felt more like a release. I transferred the glass to my other hand and watched as the blood dripped and spilled onto it making it go from the clear it began to dark, coated in my blood. I quickly pushed the glass against my uncut skin and sighed as it slid inside and the blood began to flow out. The pavement and the air around me didn't feel so cold anymore, it was actually pleasantly warm and for a moment I felt like I was back home in my bed. The thought of bed actually didn't sound all that bad, so I just let my eyes close and it felt so good. Felt so good just to let it all go and everything fade. Nothing left for me to do but to fade.

That's what she told me, and then the medication kicked in and she passed out. It's so hard to watch one who you love so much, just let everything go, what's even harder is to know that they have worked so hard to do something, to make a point and then not succeed.

Surprise, surprise, remember me? Amanda? Yeah, you got it! Kristen's little sister, who's not so little and seems to have more in common with her than she could have ever realized. I knew something was very wrong when I saw healing cuts on my sister's arms, and all her friends dying, so I followed her the night she tried to kill herself (for the third time, as it seems), I got there at what I thought was a little too late and the second I realized that she had cut herself I called the cops. The ambulances got there with the lights and sirens blaring. It was terrifying to see her blood illuminated by the flashing lights. There was so much of it everywhere, and I knew she just wouldn't make it. There was no possible way.

I rode in the ambulance with her; she looked so pale and . . . dead. The EMT kept telling me that everything would be okay, but I wasn't afraid. If she died then she got what she wanted, if she didn't, then maybe I'd get a chance to tell her exactly how I feel and how much we really do have in common.

Our parents were waiting at the hospital for us. They hugged and held me while the doctors worked on her. One of the nurses came out to give my parents her possessions. Sad thing is, all she had on her was a piece of paper. Her suicide note. I hesitate to let you read it, but seeing as you've read this far, I guess it can't hurt.

Dear Mom and Dad,

First of all you need to know that this is sort of your fault, I got sick of pretending that everything is alright, and I know that I am not needed or wanted here. I'm just another stupid teenager polluting this world. I'm pretty sure that everyone hates me, or at least can't stand me. Though, when I'm around, no one ever lets it show. If you guys had only paid a little more attention to me, instead of always worrying about yourselves, maybe you would have seen that something was wrong and could have stopped this before it got out of hand. I hate that I feel this way, but it's true. I hate the fact that I hate myself, and what I hate more is that I hate you. The one thing in my life I could have ever asked for was your love and attention. So I am ridding you of myself, the blood that I will spill is not for me but for you.

Tell Nick that I still love him, and even though he hurt me more than anyone ever has, it can't change how I feel. I know he won't miss me, but neither will you.

Please tell Mandy I'm sorry. I wish I would have known her better. I'm so, so sorry.

You might think that my life's not all that bad, and that maybe this is all just in my head. But it's too late to tell me that, by the time you find this note I will be dead. I'm sorry, so very sorry that you have to find out this way, but how else could it be done? I hope you don't cry for me, you never wasted a smile or a laugh, so for my sake and what sanity I have left, don't you dare shed a tear.

Again I say I'm sorry if I hurt you by doing this; that was not my intention. I guess in the end all I have to say is goodbye. And . . . I love you . . . I think.

~Kris

Hearing my father's cold voice read that note aloud gave me the chills. Mom was the first to cry, she began before he even started reading. I will admit, I cried too when he read the part about me. When he finished reading I could see tears in his eyes as he hugged my mother and silently they cried together. I don't know how long it was but finally the doctor came out and said everything would be okay . . . health wise. But emotionally, no one would know until she woke up. Probably she would need a lot of help is what they were predicting. Our parents took shifts in staying with her in the room, but it wasn't until they both left and I was alone with her did she wake up. She asked; begged me to get this journal for her so she could finish it. And I did. I let her finish her part, but now it's my turn.

I choose to continue where she left off. She is going to be spending, most likely, the rest of her life in therapy. She finally got what she wanted, mom and dad to pay attention to her; that leaves me out. So I choose to continue. Someone will die this month in my sister's place, whether it be me or one of my friends, it will happen. Her efforts won't go forgotten. I can promise that.